ONE AND DONE

Advance Praise for *One and Done*

"Once again, Frederick Smith continues to draw back the curtain and offer us more glimpses behind the scenes of the modern Black gay man, this time bringing us two beloved characters who deal with the real—love, sex, and all that mess in between, while still allowing them to find moments of humor and joy that all Black gay men are worthy of."—Aaron K. Foley, author, *Boys Come First*

"Grown, sexy, and a warm hug for readers with complicated pasts and busy schedules. Watching Taylor and Dustin fall in love was tender and delightful."—Katrina Jackson, author, *Office Hours* and *Sabbatical*

"*One and Done* by Frederick Smith had me hooked faster than you could say 'Beyoncé.' Actively laughing and yelling, I haven't been so quickly engaged in a book in a few reads. I loved it."—Sander Santiago, author, *Head Over Heelflip* and *One Verse Multi*

"In *One and Done*, we are invited to dance on the line between the professional and the provocative. With characters who explore the complex struggle between heart and head, Smith's novel is a slice of life portrait of what happens when ambition and romance collide."—Sheree L. Greer, author, *Let The Lover Be* and *A Return to Arms*

By the Author

Busy Ain't the Half of It
(co-authored with Chaz Lamar Cruz)

In Case You Forgot
(co-authored with Chaz Lamar Cruz)

Play It Forward

Right Side of the Wrong Bed

Down For Whatever

One and Done

ONE AND DONE

by

Frederick Smith

2024

ONE AND DONE

ISBN 13: 978-1-63679-564-5

THIS TRADE PAPERBACK ORIGINAL IS PUBLISHED BY
BOLD STROKES BOOKS, INC.
P.O. BOX 249
VALLEY FALLS, NY 12185

FIRST EDITION: JUNE 2024

CREDITS
EDITORS: JERRY WHEELER AND STACIA SEAMAN
PRODUCTION DESIGN: STACIA SEAMAN
COVER DESIGN BY RAY JEAN-GILLES

Acknowledgments

I appreciate the generosity of Chaz and Hari, who loaned me their apartment in L.A. in Summer 2023 so that I could write in a place with no distractions. *One and Done* would not have happened, or been completed, without their gift of space, place, and grace. Thank you!

I appreciate the support of my happy hour crew, also known as "The Blacks," who have become found family in San Francisco's Castro District, and whose stories and one-liners end up in my Notes app for future stories: Brian, Chris, Danique, Jonathan, L.Q., Matt, Nickolas, Omar, Pierre.

I appreciate the servers, bartenders, and neighborhood historians who fill me in on everything service industry and San Francisco: Alexis, Austin, Ben, C.J., Cherie, Cole, Danny, David, Drew, Felipe, Gage, Irwan, Jerome, Joshua, Julio, Justin, Mark, Matthew, Lee, Moses, Oscar, Q, both Sams, ShaRey, Shaun, Sheree, Summer, Treston, Trey, Vanessa, both Vinnys, and Winston. A reminder to all—tip your servers very well and they will take care of you very well!

I appreciate the dancers, performers, photographers, places, and promoters who keep San Francisco entertained during drag brunch events and more: Ashley Wevemet, Bebe Sweetbriar, Betty Fresas, Bionka Simone, Black Opal Munro, Carne Asada, Curveball, Felicia LaMar, Hera Wynn, Jaymelah Moore, Mahlae Balenciaga, Marques, Mercedez Munro, Mohammad, Ruby Red Munro, and more, Tamia, Terrill, The

Last Call, Tiv, Tony OMGF, TréBion, US, plus people I can't remember and love, so please insert your names and faves here: _____. ☺ Again, tip your performers!

I appreciate Romancelandia—the romance novel writing and reading community. Romance novels and all the virtual romance writer events got me through the 2020–2022 years when we couldn't go outside. So many writer friends (and writer friends in my mind), bookstagrammers, bookstores, and podcasts to name. But what I'll say to all is this—keep writing, keep sharing the joy of romance novels, keep giving the world happiness. The world needs love, hope, and inspiration that come from books.

Finally, thanks to educators, booksellers, and librarians who just want to open minds and hearts and bring enlightenment to the world. Books and information are the key to growing empathy and understanding, and to empowering people to make the decisions that work best for them. Please support teachers and librarians. Please support independent neighborhood bookstores.

Till the next book…Love you all!—Fred

Life in general, but especially LGBTQIA+ life, does not end at 21, 25, 30, or 40, 60, 80. It's never too late, and we're never too old, to pursue a dream or goal or to consider a new way of approaching life. I dedicate this to all who would still like to be here to lament getting older and who would love to have one more chance of going through this thing called adulting. I dedicate this to all who uplift and support our queer youth and who value and listen to our queer elders—with special reverence for all who support queer youth and elders of color.

CHAPTER ONE

Taylor

Dustin McMillan poured into my life as effortlessly as the top-shelf tequila going into the first margarita of the afternoon Markell was shaking up for me.

I was sitting alone in my usual seat adjacent to the bar at Beaux where I could chat with my best friend Markell, who was mixing up drinks for the Sunday drag brunch crowd. The DJ had just lowered the music a bit for hostess and performer Miss Coco Hydrate to get the drag brunch going. She'd asked us to get our singles out for the queens performing their interpretations of Beyoncé's *Renaissance* album—still a favorite of all the Black and Brown gays, even after all the time the album had been out, even after most of the gays had been to one of the *Renaissance* world tour concerts, and even as we eagerly anticipated Beyoncé's next project. And as I always did on Sunday afternoons, I reached into my chocolate Telfar bag and took two twenties out to change into singles for the drag performers.

"Only forty dollars?" this guy asked as he sidled up near to me and sat in an empty barstool two seats over. "*Renaissance* has sixteen tracks. And you're tipping barely two bucks per performance in expensive-ass San Francisco?"

I swung my face toward the somewhat raspy baritone

voice commenting on my tipping. For a second, I thought I was looking at myself in the mirror.

He was a Black guy, way too attractive, wearing a blue fitted suit that looked Armani and a salmon-colored button-down dress shirt with a light blue tie. Reminded me a bit of that Nate Burleson newscaster on *CBS Mornings*. Confident looking, too, like he thought he was the shit. Definitely overdressed for day drinking in the Castro. But then again, Markell often said the same about me and my Sunday Funday attire.

Not that I was sizing him up for anything beyond curiosity, we shared the same mid-to-dark brown complexion and smooth skin that looked taken care of by an aesthetician. And whereas I kept my hair in more of a clean cut, tapered low 'fro, with a small mustache and chin goatee, Two Seats Over guy was a little more rugged looking, wearing a high top natural with a fade, full beard, and mustache. His edge up was sharp and crisp.

Beyond superficial looks, that's where our similarities seemed to end. He showed some nerve. I'd never think to intrude or impose my opinion on a stranger in a bar. Work life, yes. Sunday Funday, no.

"Who asked you?" I said. Maybe I should have retorted in a nicer way, given that the number of gay Black men in the Castro, especially those who talked to other Black men in the Castro, was generally low to none. But the way he approached me, I thought my response was warranted.

"I'm just saying," Two Seats Over guy said. "You're the only other guy in here, like me, overdressed, suited, and booted. The girls are going to expect more from you...and from me."

"That's funny. I've never seen you in here before. I'm here pretty much every Sunday."

"Oh, you're a regular, then?"

"You could say that," I said. "My best friend works here."

"Oh, so everybody in here knows you're a frugal tipper? In this expensive-ass city? And what's up with this city, by the way? Is it even the destination city anymore? I mean the homeless, the mental health, the drugs. Hell, y'all even pushed Keith Lee to cancel his food critic tour. This how y'all be living in San Francisco and the Bay Area now?"

He punctuated the questions with an arrogantly radiant smile filled with Hollywood-perfect teeth. Enamored and at a loss for words at the moment, I looked down while thinking of a response, noting the stainless steel Chopard watch on his left wrist and what looked to be a Tiffany link bracelet on the right wrist. I peeped the Armani white leather sneakers and concluded his suit definitely had to be the same label as the shoes. These brands I knew by look, not because I bought them for myself, but because my parents often gifted me things I never thought or wanted to acquire for myself. Clearly, his taste and income for exorbitant goods were behind his opinions about San Francisco, a city I'd called home for about five years after leaving my family and a job I loved in Los Angeles for a better professional opportunity in the Bay Area.

I'm generally quick-witted and ready with a response for everything, so rarely does someone come for me in my professional or personal life. People who know me know winning a debate with me is hard. Except for maybe Markell's attempts to poke emotional holes in my reasons for remaining single.

"Well, what I'm *not* gonna do is buy into anything that critiques our Black woman mayor, her agenda, or her performance," I said, not really wanting to get into politics at a bar. I just wanted to talk to Markell on his Sunday shift, have my one and done cocktail, and watch some drag. But here we were. "Black women already treated as less than, and buying into that thinly veiled sexist and racist negative talk about her is a slippery slope meant to set the stage for conservatives to try and take back the city—and you know we'll never get another Black mayor again if that happens. They've already pushed enough of us Blacks out of San Francisco, Oakland, and all the Bay Area. We not doing this now. And it's not just San Francisco, in case you don't watch the news. It's all major cities."

"Point taken," Two Seats Over guy said. "I ain't even had my first drink. And I have had a day. Still don't get you off the hook for cheap tipping. Ha. Thought I forgot."

We smiled. Eyes lingered on each other. I knew what that look meant and broke eye contact. Romance was definitely not in my plan.

"I tip the girls very well, thank you," I said, hesitantly. "With cash and in other ways they need help."

"Mm-hmm, help." He looked me up and down. "That kinda help? You get down with the performers like that?"

"You don't even know me." I scanned the bar area for an empty seat, even though I hated the idea of leaving my usual place at the bar because of an annoying stranger. The nerve of him to imply help meant sex work. Not that anything was wrong with sex work. Rent's gotta be paid.

What he didn't know, not that I needed to explain anything to him, was that a lot of my professional work and community service was dedicated to helping queer, nonbinary, trans, and genderqueer people, especially Black and Brown. These groups were the ones highly likely to make up a large number of unhoused youths in the Bay Area and elsewhere. My volunteer and advocacy work was to get them connected to the services they needed. Whether their needs were food, shelter, physical health, mental health, educational, or legal, I'd volunteered on the ground and on advisory boards with organizations dedicated to the uplift of those most invisible within the LGBTQIA+ and Black communities.

And when drag queens and Black trans youth got put on the political bingo card out of the blue, I'd doubled down my support by joining the local NAACP chapter, Castro District Arts Council, and the Food, Bar, and Beverage Council to advocate for their rights. Along with giving cash and tips directly to the performers, that demonstrated my support was beyond the sex work box many tried to confine them to.

I wasn't too sure I wanted to give energy to Two Seats Over guy, who came across as conceited, opinionated, and full of himself. The kind whose good looks got him his way in his personal and professional life. I didn't really like that kind of energy in my world.

"Man, just joking," he said. He put a fist out to bump, so I extended mine back to signal a truce and, hopefully, to end the conversation. "You ain't gotta move or change seats. I just flew into San Francisco, luggage ain't make it, car service was late, and they're going to text when my hotel room is ready. It's up the street. I'm just passing time."

"All that to say you're a tourist?" I said. "If you hate it here so much, why you visiting?"

"Work. Money. A job assignment. That's it."

"Welcome, I guess. If you can play nice. And stop talking shit about my city since you're making money here."

"Point taken. Thanks for welcoming me, man. I'm familiar with the area somewhat, so I'm entitled to talk shit. But I'll quit. I'm D.J."

"Oh, I see. I'm Taylor."

"Taylor? As in 'beautiful gowns' Taylor?"

"You got jokes like Aretha Franklin, huh?"

"So, what's behind your name? What the hell kinda Black family names a kid Taylor?"

"The kind that named me Taylor, I guess."

"*Doctor* Taylor, if you want to be more specific," Markell interrupted, thankfully, as he made his way back to the bar, vogueing quickly past the performer who was in the middle of doing Beyoncé's "I'm That Girl." For a thick and muscular guy who had formerly done drag in his twenties and early thirties before giving up entertaining, Markell could still easily jump in and around the current girls performing at Beaux during his bartending shift.

In between making my margarita, mixing others' drinks, and delivering mimosas and food orders to the various Sunday Funday groups at tables around the club, Markell had grabbed some casual clothes out his locker in the back—a green T-shirt and light blue denim jacket he'd wanted me to change into, as I was, as usual, overdressed for Sunday Funday. He set the clothes in the empty seat between me and Two Seats Over guy.

"Here's your drink you ordered from the app," Markell said and sat something dark on ice in front of D.J. "Doc, I can get you into the staff lounge if you want to change clothes."

"You changing, *Doctor* Taylor?" D.J. said, looking me up and down again. "You look fine as you are."

I hated when Markell, or anyone else outside of the university where I worked, emphasized my academic title. I knew they were proud. I was proud, too, knowing I'd accomplished something less than two percent of the population had achieved. But now wasn't the time for formalities. Not among bar friends and strangers.

"Aww, man, look at you...another suited and booted kinda guy," Markell said to D.J. "I swear y'all act like you've never been to a club for day drinking before."

"And you're?"

"I'm Markell. I'm a bartender, mixologist, sometimes

deejay, barback, whatever they need here, and best friend of Doc."

"That's what's up," D.J. said. "I'm D.J. And yep, the kinda Black family that names people D.J., C.J., B.J., and all that… based on who the daddy is. Not that you asked, Doc."

"I didn't, and please don't call me Doc." I turned to Markell. "He's visiting San Francisco. But didn't say from where or how long. Right?"

"What's with all the questions, Gayle King?" D.J. said. He laughed and poked at my ribs to see if he'd get a reaction out of me and flashed that million-dollar smile again. "Just joking."

"Get him away from me, Markell," I said, trying not to smile but realizing I was. I don't drink much, so the one margarita already had me on the edge of giddy. Not my intention. "Eighty-six him. D.J.'s been coming for me since he got here. He don't even know me like that."

"What's going on?" Markell asked. D.J. and I squinted eyes at each other and said nothing. "I'ma need y'all to get a shot and loosen up the tension."

"I ain't tense," D.J. and I said at the same time, with the same raised voice pitch. Laughed.

"Since you're obviously not changing, then, let me take these clothes back and I'll let y'all work out whatever's…um, whatever."

"There is no whatever," D.J. and I said, again, in unison.

And then again, "Whatever."

"I'll be back," Markell said, heading to the back of the bar as Miss Coco Hydrate announced a short intermission before she'd be back to perform "Alien Superstar."

D.J. scooted over a seat and was now directly next to me. A waft of sandalwood floated toward me. Smelled nice on him.

"Hope you don't mind," he said, as Beyoncé's "Texas Hold 'Em" started playing over the speakers. "I wanna hear what you say. I ain't a kid anymore. I don't feel like yelling over the music while talking to you."

In my mind, D.J. was getting a little too comfortable and too fast with me. Casually chatting with some of the Beaux regulars sitting solo around and across the bar was more my style. Anything more intimate—not.

❖

Weird as it may sound, I enjoyed my solo outings on Sunday at Beaux, rather than being with large groups like I used to do back in my twenties. Beaux was one of the more popular spots in the Castro District, the predominantly queer neighborhood of San Francisco, among many that people hung out in for Sunday Funday. As Markell described from his work there, and I observed for myself when I'd stop by to visit Markell, Beaux was a spot with three distinct personalities: the nighttime dancing club for twentysomethings; the happy hour and chill hang out after work bar for those skewing thirty, forty, fiftysomething; and the drag brunch crowd, which brought together the young and the young at heart of all demographics.

I loved Sunday in general because it was the one day of the week I set aside *not* to do any work. Or, at least, not to do *much* work, besides glancing at my Monday meetings schedule to make sure I was mentally and professionally prepared for the week ahead. Sunday morning and afternoon was my time to splurge and to spend time on myself doing whatever I wanted. Mostly, a day of rest.

Usually, the day'd begin with a video chat with my parents in Los Angeles before they left for services, which I would then livestream so I could feel connected to my family and to our longtime church, Faithful Central. Sometimes I'd skip the livestream and head over to Third Baptist, the oldest Black church in San Francisco. Then a late morning or early afternoon gym trip and massage while the cleaning person tidied up my apartment and did my week's laundry. And if I felt like it, maybe I'd do a farmers market visit and some meal prep before catching a Lyft over to the Castro District in the late afternoon to see Markell during his Sunday bartending shift and catch the Sunday Funday drag show.

It was the one day of the week I allowed myself to have a drink, see my best friend, and join the other bar friends and acquaintances who sat solo, like I did, near the bartenders' wells. Unlike the groups of straight women, gay men, and genderqueers of all persuasions sitting at tables around the perimeter of the club or the glass-front and street-side windows, the solos and I were planning to be on our way home by five, maybe six at the latest, in order to wind down and get ready for the workday on Monday.

Knowing Markell couldn't spend all his work shift entertaining me, sometimes I'd bring my tablet and glance at work to pass time. I'd lie and say I was gaming, though Markell knew I was not good at lying or playing video games.

A Monday state holiday coming, César Chávez Day, I'd spent a little more time preparing for my upcoming Tuesday work just before that day's Sunday Funday outing.

Tuesday, I knew, was going to be a doozy.

It was our first meetings, with an "s," with the academic accreditation team visiting the campus where I worked—California University Lake Merced. That day, a team of a dozen or so educational leaders were on the way for a few weeks to audit the report I had spent much of the last year and a half writing. Now, after leading several hundred hours of work, writing the report, and coordinating dozens of campus work groups, all while navigating the egos of academia, I knew this visit was a make-or-break moment for my career.

For if successful with the university accreditation process, I was on the verge of crossing a hurdle to my next career aspiration—to advance from my vice president role and become a university president. Not only a president, but the first Black, openly gay, and relatively young-for-the-profession college president I knew of.

Prior to heading out that day, I smiled, thinking about my parents and how I'd made them happy and proud with my achievements. I scrolled the tablet one last time reviewing the Tuesday agendas. Everything looked set. Perfect. *Virgo* perfect.

❖

Apparently, I'd been daydreaming and gotten distracted in the moment. D.J. pointed to my drink and asked, "What you drinking?" As if he couldn't tell it was a margarita, even with the salt and tajín on the rim. I snapped back into the present.

"I'm a tequila person. A margarita."

D.J. smiled and laughed. "You're not one of those Casamigos gays, huh? I know about y'all. The stories I've witnessed and heard from my friends."

"Oh, you must have a messy crew. Wherever you're from, D.J.?"

"I don't do messy," he said. "Though I've been messed over."

"Oh, have you? Wanna talk about it?"

"Are you a therapist, Doc? Because I ain't wasting time talking about heaux, exes, almost fiancés, or anyone else at the moment."

"Fine, just offering to lend an ear," I said. "Black men are rare in this city. Just here to help. If you need."

"Like you offer help to the drag performers?" D.J. said, inquisitively cocking his head to the side. "I'm just kidding. You don't look like a heaux or like you been ran through your friend circles."

"And if I was 'ran through,' as you say, that would be okay," I said as I finished the last of my margarita. Definitely sure I'd be one and done and out soon, given the company. "Sex positivity. Accept people as they are."

"Yeah, until you get fucked over," he said, looking anxiously around the bar and then at his phone. "Anyway, you want another one? On me?"

"I'm just a one and done kinda guy."

"Your friend Markell offered us shots."

"And like I said, one and done is enough for me."

"Monday's a holiday, Doc. I'm not working. I hope you ain't working."

"I'm not."

"Then sit and have a drink with me," D.J. said, nodding and raising his glass. "I mean, it's not a good look being a solo guy sitting at the bar alone."

"I do it every Sunday."

"This ain't no ordinary Sunday," he said, smiling and winking. His voice took on a playful and flirty tone. "You sitting with me today, Doc."

"You kinda conceited, huh?"

"Kinda? Yeah."

"I don't do conceited. Nor cocky. Nor ego."

"But you *do* do mature, I hope."

"Depends on how mature, D.J." I looked him up and down to try and figure out if we might be in the same age range.

With surgeries, weight-loss prescriptions, fillers, dye jobs, hair plugs, and other procedures more and more common, these days it was hard to figure out by looking at someone how old they might be, despite the gift of melanin and Mother Nature on the side of Black people. "Monitoring your blood pressure mature? Metabolism slowing down mature? Getting your first colonoscopy mature? Shingles vaccine mature? Erectile dysfunction mature? Shall I go on?"

"Ahh. Very clever, Doc. Using your medical knowledge to guess my age."

"Not a medical doctor, but that's for another time and place." I looked at his empty glass and wondered how long it'd be before Markell returned. "So, how mature? Does your birth year start with nineteen or twenty?"

"Ha. You got jokes, Doc. I *know* I don't look like someone born in the two thousands."

"You never know."

"I'm a bae, but definitely not a baby gay."

"So, how mature, then?"

"Somewhere around that first colonoscopy mature," D.J. said with a laugh. "But only because my father...anyway. Not even close for shingles mature. And as Black people, we all gotta keep track of blood pressure no matter what age."

"Gotcha. Same here. Except my father didn't..."

"Oh, mine didn't either. He still around somewhere. He was just a rolling stone, and all I need from him is to know how his DNA is gonna impact me. You feel me?"

"Sorry to hear, D.J."

"Back to the topic at hand. Black obviously don't crack."

"That's the truth."

"I got a good doctor who keeps me young," D.J. said, and he gave me the up-and-down glance once again, as if he were savoring one of the brown liquors stacked in front of the mirrored wall behind the bar. "Just kidding."

I smiled. Flattered. But not taking the bait from D.J. Relationships were not part of the personal or professional plan. Not when being a potential college president one day was on the line. That career move required focus.

Before intentionality was a part of my personal and career plans, I'd had my share of thot moments, situationships, and one-night relationships that added nothing to the overall trajectory of my life. My days of one-and-done bar hookups were a lifetime ago, when I was a young, slender, tender ingenue on the scene, and they were easier to attain and do.

"But anyway, to answer your question, D.J., I don't have to work tomorrow," I said. "So, I'll have that shot Markell offered. I'll take care of my own drinks and tab, though, thank you."

"I wasn't offering. Yet."

"That's okay, D.J." I turned to Markell, who had returned to his bar station. "Hey, Markell. I'll take that shot now. You know my brand, and then another of my usuals, on my tab. And on his tab, D.J. is having…?"

"Hennessy Sidecar for my drink. And another Hennessy, chilled, for my shot."

"Speaking of heaux tales," I said and grimaced. "You and that dark liquor. I'm not judging."

"Yeah, you are judging, Doc, and that's all right, given the way I came at you," D.J. said. "You're cool people. Too bad I'm just in and out for a quick consulting job in San Francisco."

"How long you here, did you say?"

"Probably four weeks. Maybe five. I think. Depends on how easy the client is with this project."

"Good luck with that. We like easy, not hard."

D.J. and I locked eyes, and if I was alone, I would have pinched myself for being so salacious with my word choices.

"Sometimes hard is easy...and good."

I looked away; thought I might be blushing from D.J.'s obvious flirtation. Though people had shown interest in subtle ways with me, at times, being flirted with by someone so forward was something of a distant memory. People in my circles, primarily academic ones, flirted at yearly professional conferences with each other, and that was flirtation primarily with citations, discourse, reading lists, ideas, and sizing up whose research or publications were the most current and cutting edge. Academic rock stars were the people I'd generally had as a type, if I had a type to reference when asked.

Markell interrupted and slid a tray of drinks in front of us. "Cheers, fellas. To *Renaissance*. To Sunday Funday."

D.J., Markell, and I tapped glasses, tapped the counter, made the required eye contact for shots, and threw them back. We all made that gagging sound and swallowed our chasers.

"I'm done," I said. "No more."

"You've gagged on far less and far more, Taylor," Markell said to me and laughed. Years of being best friends since our elementary school days in L.A. behind us, we both knew the conquest and body count stories of our lives.

"Oh, you a freaky doc, hmm, Doc? I like that."

"Everybody got a past," I said. "No shame."

"And a present." D.J. laughed, smirked, and locked eyes with me. "I hope."

"No future for someone in town for just a few weeks." I wondered why I couldn't keep from feeling charmed by this stranger in a bar. Such a cliché. I was definitely too mature for this kind of bar flirtation, and certainly D.J. was, too.

"Oh, so a present then, Doc?" D.J. smiled. "A present for me?"

I unfixed my gaze from D.J. for fear of giving any impression of being interested and turned back to Markell at his station behind the bar. "What was in that shot again?"

"Shot," Markell said, and laughed heartily while mixing up another round of drinks. "Want another while I got your tequila out?"

"No, no, no, no, no, no, no," I said, shaking my head, each "no" getting louder with each head movement. "I'm done with shots today. Gonna stay till the show ends and then I'm out. Might even leave after they do 'Virgo's Groove.'"

"Cheap *and* leaving the show early," D.J. said. "Ha. I see you."

"Oh, do you?"

"I'm just joking with you, Doc."

Markell slid D.J. and me another round of drinks and looked at his watch.

"I'm down to do Sunday Funday with you after I'm off, Taylor," Markell said. "You, too, D.J., if you want. Since neither of you working tomorrow and you're new in town, D.J., we can show you around the Castro."

After thirty-plus years of being best friends, I knew this barhopping invitation was Markell's way of attempting to matchmake, to forge some kind of connection between D.J. and me beyond the moment. He'd been doing this since we first figured out our sexuality during our classmate days at Loyola High School in L.A. First, trying to fix me up with his closeted athlete teammates, then through the years as we both pursued our own personal and professional goals. As if I wasn't adult enough to pursue someone of interest.

Markell mouthed the word "typo" to me, which, in our secret best friend language, was an abbreviation that stood for "take your pants off," meaning Markell thought D.J. was fine as hell and that I should go for it.

"New in town? Bitch, are you for real?"

D.J., Markell, and I turned around to see who'd interrupted our bar-side conversation. Manessa DelRey. One of the drag performers at Sunday brunches throughout the Castro neighborhood and someone I'd helped out financially and academically in their time at the university. They were tall, bold, Black, and beautiful in a yellow metallic gown, makeup and face card impeccably drawn on, and a blond Beyoncé sew-in that contrasted and complemented their dark brown skin. They were loud. Generally, it was impossible to be even louder than the drag performers' music, but the sound barrier was meant to be shattered on this day. I'd known Manessa for a couple years since my move to San Francisco. But how did they know D.J., this tourist and stranger who was both annoying and intriguing to me?

"Let's take this outside," D.J. said and stood up, looking a little nervous, the color draining from his smooth brown skin, the baritone still baritoning in his voice.

"Everything okay?" I asked.

"Everything's fine," D.J. said.

"We can keep this inside, right here, right now, Junior."

Markell and I mouthed "Junior?" to each other. It felt like a moment made for the *Karamo* show. Exasperatedly, I shrugged my shoulders, rolled my eyes, and grimaced at Markell. In my mind, I knew I'd been right all along to focus on my career and no possibility of a relationship at this point. And especially now, with D.J. or Junior or whoever he was, and this loudmouth confronting him, presenting as a top-shelf kinda guy, but all along being no more than a two-for-one well-drink special.

CHAPTER TWO

Dustin

I loved my cousin Man-Man. I had to. We grew up together on the same block in Oakland. And at one point we were really close since we bonded as the only openly queer people we knew of in the family.

But I did not like them. Nor did I appreciate the way Man-Man, who was now going by their new performer name Manessa DelRey, made a fool of me in front of Taylor, who I was sure would never want to see me again. Not only had I misled Doc about my name—I mean D.J. is short for Dustin Jr., i.e., Junior, named for the man whose genetics made me—but beyond the name, I had not been forthcoming about a lot of my life, including that I'd grown up in the Bay Area and up until a few years ago had lived in San Francisco. Not that Taylor, nor any stranger in a bar, was entitled to know anything beyond surface-level details about anyone upon a first meeting.

I stood in the small bathroom of my room in the Hotel Castro, face above the sink, tasting the remnants of too many Hennessy shots. Fortysomething was too old to be downing shots and drinking like a college coed. Wished I'd eaten something. Prayed I wouldn't throw up. Wouldn't have had that much to drink if not for the so-called family popping up and fucking up my game. Forgot how small San Francisco was.

Gay San Francisco even smaller. Splashed some cold water over my face with one hand while bracing myself against the wall with the other because the room felt like it was moving around me, spinning like a tea cups ride at a Disney amusement park. I replayed everything that happened before I got too shit-faced to try and hang out with Taylor and Markell. Not that they would have wanted to continue hanging out with me.

❖

Fuck, that man is fine, I said to myself as I walked randomly into Beaux while going north on Market Street in the Castro. Through the large street-facing windows I saw the Black bartender, who turned out to be Markell, shaking up drinks, and heard Beyoncé blasting on the inside-and-outside-the-club speakers. But it was seeing Taylor, overdressed and looking all nerdy like me in his black polo shirt and tan khaki slacks, almost like my twin and sitting alone at the end of the bar that caught my eye. He looked like an actor on one of the soaps I grew up watching. Taylor's smell was clean and fresh, like soap and cocoa butter, and his skin was glistening, smooth, and lustrous. It was not like me at all to be mesmerized at first sight. My style, generally, was to play it cool. Until the liquor kicked in and threw me off my game.

But like they used to teach us back in elementary school, if you can imagine it, you can have it. I was determined I was going to have Taylor in my hotel bed for the night or at some point during my four- or five-week work assignment in San Francisco. Something inside me, though, after meeting him wanted more than one night—maybe, at minimum, Taylor as a reliable and steady sex partner while visiting San Francisco; at the aspirational level, something beyond a hit-and-quit. I didn't know what was coming over me.

The whole time I was there playing reindeer games with Taylor, I was a nervous wreck inside. And I was so on edge that if I moved the right way, depending on who was looking down at my tight blue suit pants, Taylor would see just how excited and brick I was for him. Taylor and his shy, quiet yet witty comebacks to my conceit were a turn-on. Fire. I fantasized what our coming together in bed would be. Even though he looked like he could pass for my twin, which was a shallow and narcissistic turn-on to me already, it was his yin to my yang, his water to my oil that made me want to eat him up the first chance I got.

That was until Man-Man, who I didn't recognize at first underneath the makeup, hair, and body padding, approached and interrupted. No one, though, could mistake Man-Man's voice, even when living life as performer Manessa DelRey.

"How long you been in town?" Man-Man asked.

"I just landed a couple hours ago."

"How come you ain't tell nobody you was in the Bay Area, Junior?" Man-Man flicked their hair and popped their tongue. "You think you too good for us now or something?"

"I don't go by Junior anymore, Man-Man. I use D.J. in social settings, Dustin in work settings now."

"Ooh." Tongue pop. Eye roll. "'Dustin in work settings.' Aunt Kim know you don't go by Junior no more?"

"She knows. She forgets. I'm not repeating myself a million times to my mama for stuff she should remember."

"Well." Tongue pop. Eye roll. Hair flip. "Bitch, just like I don't go by Man-Man anymore, I go by Manessa now. Don't use my deadname, and I won't use yours."

"Fair enough."

"Still talking all proper and shit like you did when we was growing up in West Oakland…'fair enough.' Sounding like my boy Taylor over here."

And Manessa pointed to Taylor.

What I did not want was my cousin bringing Taylor into any of our personal family drama. And I did not want to be reminded of, let alone for anyone to know about, my life coming of age in Oakland. Too many memories of survival, struggle, and loss. Watching my mom raise my brother and me on next to nothing but getting the ends met via the strange and various men, including my DNA provider, who came in and out of our house. Me cutting grass and delivering newspapers to help keep lights on and to buy school clothes for my younger brother, Dorian, named after his father. Feeling violated when the house would get broken into, but feeling even more violated when my mom would take my hard-earned cash from a not-so-hidden spot in the room I shared with my brother. Being okay with the realization that I was gay early on in life, but knowing it was smarter to keep it quiet in order to avoid being bullied and having my ass kicked on the daily by classmates, neighbors, and family. Thanking God daily for the four-year full-ride academic and track-and-field scholarship that got me out of Oakland, onto a safe college campus, and onto a road of social mobility and financial stability that eventually transitioned me into the role of the family's ATM—my mom's for everything she needed money for, and Dorian's for miscellaneous court fees, lawyers, and electronic fund transfers to him at the prison in Solano County.

Stuff I didn't like to think about.

I assumed Taylor was a person with manners, when he acknowledged Manessa pointing at him, but continued *pretending* to be in conversation with Markell. Taylor didn't know I could see him and Markell making eyes at each other. Although I couldn't read their minds, I knew how best friends could be with each other. Nosy bitches, I thought to myself, feeling that the alcohol was getting to me pretty quickly.

By that point, Taylor and Markell had to be aware of my real name, that I had a cousin who happened to perform drag at Beaux and in the Castro District—random, I swear, I ain't even know—my roots were in the Bay Area, and that I wasn't some tourist stranger sitting in a bar. Damned and clocked by them for sure.

"Markell," Manessa shouted over the girl performing Beyoncé's "Church Girl." "Can you get me a shot? You know what I like. And one for my cousin here. Whatever he drinking. And one for my boy, the quiet one, here."

"I'm good, Man…Manessa," I said.

"You gotta do a shot with me," they said and did a little body roll and shimmer. "I'm about to do 'Virgo's Groove' in a few minutes. That's my favorite on *Renaissance*, by the way. Don't no other girls get to do that song but me in the Castro. You gotta stay."

"I'm just passing time till my hotel room is ready."

"Bitch, you staying." Tongue pop. Eye roll. Finger nail clap in sync with each syllable. "No one else in the fam cares to come and see this part of my life. You and I used to be like this close back in the day."

Manessa reached out and did the Black person three-part handshake most of us grew up doing whenever we'd acknowledge another Black person who was new or familiar, but definitely on friendly terms with.

"I know. I remember."

"And why you ain't staying at Aunt Kim's since you in town? Too good to stay in Oakland?"

"I got a short-term consulting gig here. I'm not moving back. It's more convenient to stay close to where I'm contracted to work."

"Well, I commute from Oakland to the Castro almost every damn day, so I know you can do it," Manessa said.

"Anyway, West Oakland changing. White people moving in by the hundreds. And your mama got the house remodeled. Plenty of room there if you choose to stay or pay a visit."

"I know, Manessa. I paid for the renovations. Per usual."

"Well, the family, we was all over there after early church service ended today *per usual.*" Tongue pop. Eye roll. Hair flip. "Aunt Kim made a buffet for the family. Damn, your mama can cook. I ain't eat, though, but I took a plate to go, since I knew I'd be performing today. Ain't nobody knew you were in town, Junior, Dustin, whatever you go by. Otherwise, we woulda made a McMillan family party out of your arrival since it's a three-day weekend. But no one knows you here but me. When you gone tell your mama you in town?"

"I'll get around to it."

Again, I saw Taylor and Markell look at each other, and I knew I was losing points fast with Taylor. All I wanted to do was continue the conversation with Doc. I wanted to get to know him more. If only Manessa knew how to keep their mouth shut in public. Big personality and mouth back in the day and big personality and mouth presently. Per usual.

"Hmmmph." Tongue pop. "Well, speaking of your mama, when you get around to it, you can pay me back the money I gave Aunt Kim to get a new 'frigerator last month."

"I gave her three grand when she called me up crying about how her old one gave out, and it wasn't even that old. I even got her a credit line for appliances in case she needed more."

Tongue pop. Eye roll. Hair flip.

"Well, I guess Aunt Kim played both of us. She stay on a turnaround trip to play the slots at Cache Creek."

"Well, damn. That's my mama. Can't trust her with money."

"But we love her just the same."

Markell slid shots across the counter to Manessa, Taylor, and me. We all downed them, except for Taylor, who was looking a little judgey as he pushed his shot back toward Markell.

"I'll take it, then," I said, smiling at Taylor in hopes he knew I knew our chemistry was fizzling but that I didn't want it to die completely. Downed it. Started feeling really woozy and hot. Hadn't eaten since the airport in Chicago before the flight to San Francisco. I meant it when I said, "No more. I'm done."

"You are," Taylor said low enough to be courteous, yet shady and loud enough for me to overhear what he intended for me to hear. Definitely felt I'd lost my chance, though we hadn't really had a chance to go beyond small talk in a bar. Something about Taylor smoldered in my mind.

"Well, anyway, Junior, you can transfer the money to me now." Tongue pop. Eye roll. Hair flip. Snapped me out of daydreaming about Taylor and what a mess I was making of myself and of our meet-cute moment. Manessa took out their phone. "Here's my app to transfer. By the way, one grand goes to me and one grand goes to Silas."

Even more McMillan family drama. I wondered why the fuck Manessa was still in contact with my ex. So, that's exactly what I asked.

"Why the *fuck* are you still in contact with my ex, Manessa? And why the *fuck* is he giving refrigerator money to my mama? Does Silas even have a thousand dollars?"

For a couple years, I'd been through with Silas, this sexy, biracial go-go dancer I'd met and flirted with after a night of heavy drinking in the South of Market gay bars right before the pandemic hit. I was mesmerized with him as he worked the pole and rocked and rolled his body on the metal box for the crowd, all the time his eyes on me. Tipped him a few too many twenties, which bought me some conversation and time with him in between sets. Let him come to my place that night, back when I had my condo in the Dogpatch neighborhood of San Francisco. Showed me how good a private dancer he was all that weekend. When the world shut down that Monday, I let him pack up his room full of stuff at the place he was staying, and he was living with me on Tuesday.

Initially, not a problem. Silas said go-go dancing was more lucrative and engaged his creative side, but with bars and clubs closed down indefinitely, he'd try to put his teaching credentials to use by getting an online gig with the San Francisco Unified School District.

While I worked remotely in a makeshift workspace I carved out in my, then our, bedroom, the only online searching Silas did was for what was streaming on one of the many services I'd subscribed to. I worked. Silas streamed. I cleaned. Silas streamed. I cooked. Silas streamed. I washed clothes. Silas streamed. I paid the household bills. Silas collected unemployment and pandemic checks for artists, paid nothing on the bills, and streamed.

Then the presidential election happened later that year. His mail had been coming to my place regularly after many months of sheltering-in-place, and I mistakenly opened what I thought was my absentee ballot but wasn't. Turned out Silas was registered a Republican. Also turned out Silas had voted for and planned to vote again for Forty-Five. I'd been fucking a fucking gay Republican. I'd never known a gay Republican, a Black Republican, nor a Black gay Republican. That had never been on my wish list.

Our pandemic romance came to a screeching halt. Like that. I stopped sleeping with Silas. Moved him and his suitcases to the living room, where he could stream to his heart's content until he could find a job, get his own place, or wait out shelter-in-place to do all of the above. Soon as outside opened up, I asked for a transfer to the Chicago office of my former consulting firm. I moved without letting anyone know I was leaving the Bay Area, and let Silas keep the Dogpatch place.

Silas met Manessa through the small industry of gay club performers, dancers, servers, and bartenders. How Silas met my mom, I didn't even want to know.

Maybe my response was brash. Manessa was, after all, my cousin.

I could see Taylor pretending *not* to be in the personal conversation I was having with Manessa.

"D.J., Dustin…come on, lead with love," Taylor said, lots of compassion in his voice, hands clasped like a steeple. Seemed like such a sweetheart, which endeared me more. He turned to Manessa and me. "Manessa's about to perform, and you getting all heated with them is not the move. Manessa, I'll app you the money later. You go and have a good performance. 'Virgo's Groove' is my favorite, too."

"Taylor," I said. "You don't have to. You don't know our situation."

"But I do know Manessa, and regardless of what's happening with you two, it's not worth killing the vibe," Taylor said, and then he turned to Manessa and grabbed their hands. "Don't worry about it. We'll work it out. Go. Have fun. Consider this tips for the next year."

Manessa and I parted ways with an awkward silence and no real goodbye as they left to get prepared for their performance. I turned back to Taylor, feeling embarrassed by the whole scene between Manessa and me.

"You're such a saint, Taylor," I said. "I'll give Manessa the money."

I didn't know what kind of doctor Taylor was. But even if

he was a medical one, I knew how expensive life was in San Francisco. Handing out two grand to Manessa had to be an imposition on Taylor's budget. Hell, he'd barely planned to hand out forty dollars to the performers that day.

"All good," Taylor said. "Don't worry about it."

"Doc, come on. Why are you so kind and generous?"

"No reason not to be."

"I could kiss you." I stared into his eyes, letting them linger in a way that conveyed gratitude and attraction. I leaned in. I'd hoped he couldn't tell how tipsy I'd become off the Hennessy. "Can I?"

Taylor smirked. "I would have said yes maybe just a few moments before the incident with Manessa. But now, the answer is a resounding no."

❖

I continued looking in the hotel bathroom mirror and bracing myself against the wall. I grabbed one of the plush hotel towels to dry my face.

I replayed the day over and over, wondering what and how I could have done things differently. Everything was just too random and too lined up for a perfect storm—the randomness of walking into Beaux when there were dozens of other bars in the Castro to pass time; meeting Taylor; Manessa working and performing there, our McMillan family drama, the refrigerator and the ex; my conceited act while flirting with Taylor; my asshole behavior with Manessa; and Taylor's rejection. The rejection hurt the most because of how saintly and sanctimonious Taylor was about it. Still, something about Taylor lingered, and I knew I'd have no other chance to shoot my shot with him.

"Fuck," I said out loud to myself, reflecting on the day,

certain that the occupants adjacent to me in this boutique Hotel Castro would wonder what was going on in my room. I tossed the moist towel out the bathroom onto the bed, just a few feet away, where the blue suit, dress shirt, and tie I'd had on earlier were also strewn.

Little would my hotel neighbors know I was on the journey to a bad hangover, despite downing a pack of BC headache powder from the Walgreens down the street.

But worse than that, little would they know that I'd let Taylor, who I thought might have the potential to be the one, go because of my own stupidity and drunkenness.

Luckily, I'd have a full holiday Monday to recover, sleep until whenever with the blackout blinds fully drawn shut, unpack, and order food from the hotel's Lobby Bar. At some point, I'd need to review documents related to my new temporary San Francisco gig that would begin in a couple days—ugh, life as a project manager and consultant. Another city. Another hotel. Another project. Another few weeks before moving on to the next one.

Unfortunately, I thought, there'll never be another Taylor.

CHAPTER THREE

Taylor

"Doc, you'll never guess who stopped by Beaux yesterday looking for you during my happy hour shift."

Not that I wanted to guess on a Tuesday morning that felt like a Monday due to a three-day weekend. But there I was, starting my morning off with a phone call from Markell.

I was walking around Lake Merced to the campus of California University just as the sun was starting to peek through the clouds. I lived in an apartment on the southwest side of San Francisco in an area many overlooked and did not realize was part of the city limits. I had views of Lake Merced to the east and the Pacific Ocean to the west. The university sat on the east side of the lake, and thus my morning commute was a nice twenty-minute walk from apartment to office door.

It was a big day, the start of the university accreditation visit I'd prepared for for almost a year. I wanted to arrive before the accreditation team visiting campus did. No holiday or three-day weekend for me. I'd spent most of it preparing so that my team and I could make our best impression on day one of the multiweek process.

I turned off the latest episode of the *Gettin' Grown* podcast I was listening to in order to take Markell's call. He sounded eager to fill me in on what I'd missed at Beaux on the Monday holiday happy hour shift.

"Don't tell me. That D.J., Dustin, Junior…whatever his name is?" I could see my breath forming little steam clouds in the chilly morning air.

"Yeah, him," Markell said. "Makes you wonder what's up with all the aliases."

"Markell, I really don't care," I said. "The accreditation visit starts today in a couple hours. Last thing I want to talk about is Dustin and his conceited, obnoxious ass."

"I'ma make it quick, Doc. I'm about to get off the train," Markell said, his phone service going in and out as the MUNI operator announced the Powell Street stop. Markell's morning gig was at the downtown Equinox, where he worked as a personal trainer and massage therapist for the techies and venture capitalists still working and living in the city. "Homie tried to play it off that he was just walking up Market Street to pick up a food order, and again happened to walk by Beaux. But I could tell what he was trying to do. Or who he was looking for. He asked about you."

"Good for him, he asked about me," I said, scooting over for a couple of joggers headed toward me on the pedestrian path. I smiled at the joggers, feeling kinda flattered Dustin had asked about me. "Was he sober this time?"

"Didn't drink a thing. Though I offered to comp him a drink or a shot."

"Well, that's sobering news."

"Felt bad for him, you know, Doc," Markell said. "I mean, small world him being cousins with Manessa DelRey—the ex, the fridge, and all the rest of the *Days of Our Lives* unfolding in front of us. I know he was just trying to make an impression on you, even with his 'conceit,' as you call it, and it went nuclear fast. I don't think you shoulda rejected him so quickly. You feel me? He's definitely a typo."

"And a liar."

"Is a lie of omission really a lie? Especially to a stranger in a bar? Everyone's pretending and fronting in a bar. That's Bar Psychology 101."

"You're funny, Markell, but I'm not interested."

"I'm just saying."

"And I am just saying, once again…"

"Everybody needs a maintenance check, Doc," Markell said, laughing. "But I know you focused on becoming a university president one day, so whatever. Presidents need love, too."

"I'm good being solo. Thank you."

"Well, if he stops by Beaux again while he's in town, I might slip him my information. Or my Instagram."

"I don't think your husband would appreciate that, Markell, even though everyone in San Francisco is in an open relationship, it seems."

"I was just joking," he said. "No one in the world makes me happier than my Nate. I want that kinda happiness for you, bestie."

Markell and I had been like brothers since we were six or seven years old. My mom had been Markell's first grade teacher when she taught in L.A. Unified, long before transitioning to teaching and administration in university life. Markell's mom and mine had taken a liking to each other, due, primarily, to raising boys around the same age in L.A. and having similar life experiences. After learning that he was home alone until the late evening hours when Markell's mom would finish her jobs, she would let him come to our house with her after school. Those daily after-school visits evolved into invitations to family gatherings, weekend sleepovers, and summer vacations, bringing Markell and me closer as playmates, friends, and childhood confidantes. When his mother got sick and her health declined quickly, my parents decided to foster and then raise him as their own after his mother passed. The gay identity piece came way later, during high school and college, with Markell always looking out for me, my well-being, and my love life.

I was glad Markell and I weren't video chatting, or else he would have seen me rolling my eyes at him. He was always encouraging me to get into a romantic relationship, as if one just wished for a relationship and, poof, it happened. I could count on several fingers and toes the number of people Markell tried to connect me with and bar patrons who he said wanted to get with me. Not that I was against love, connection, sex, and romance. My focus was always academics and my professional life, and if something happened to come along, it would come along. Last thing I needed was a man and a relationship to distract me from my future campus presidency aspirations.

"Thank you, Markell. I appreciate that."

"Just looking out," Markell said. "Anyway, I ain't want nothing. Just to share that tea about Dustin. Good luck with the accreditation blah blah blah. Let me know how day one goes."

"Will do."

Markell had some nerve, I thought, putting D.J./Jr./Dustin on my mind this morning of all mornings. After ending the call, I put some lo-fi beats on my headphones to help me concentrate on the final few minutes of my walk. I knew a tough day was ahead.

As much as pop culture and people outside the field may have thought the world of academia was full of kind, enlightened people seeking truth and knowledge, my experience with academic life was sometimes conflicted and nothing like that. For the most part, I'd had great students, colleagues, and supervisors. But there was a side of education that many did not see. Students and parents yelled. People emailed the most unthinkable judgments and opinions. Peers appeared nice but did mean things. Work got stolen and credited to other people. Decisions challenged. Microaggressions daily. Professional jealousy abounded. Luckily my parents, both having served as professors, department chairs, and other types of college administrators in their respective careers, helped guide me through numerous dilemmas. But their main advice to me was to always lead with love, assertiveness, kindness, and compassion, and those qualities will lead to the right decision.

My morning walks to work helped center me for whatever challenges would come my way.

As I approached the front door of Merced Hall and rode the elevator to the fifth floor, I took the headphones out my ears and put them back into their case. Ready for showtime, which would begin in a little bit. Loved that I arrived early and in good spirits.

"I see you're running on CP time again, Taylor James. The accreditation team has been here and waiting since seven this morning."

Wes Jenkins had a smug look on his face. He sipped from his maize and blue Michigan coffee mug. Wes looked accreditation visit ready, I had to admit, with a fitted chocolate brown suit that matched his skin tone and round designer frames. Wes was what we'd call a Carlton, with his somewhat whiny voice tone, overly enunciated words, chemically processed shiny hair, and a face devoid of any mustache or beard. I never saw Wes with anyone Black either at or outside of work. In most of his office photos and social media posts, he even seemed to take pride in being the one happy Black in the pictures.

Wes and I had always had some kind of weird energy between us, starting when the university president had appointed me over Wes as a vice president almost five years earlier. Some said it was a role Wes thought would automatically be his since he'd been at the campus many years before my arrival. Markell and I thought it might have been that weird I-want-to-be-the-only-Black-or-gay-in-the-room competitiveness that made Wes see me as a threat at work. Not that I needed anyone to call me Dr. James or Vice President James, or any other title, but I always felt some kind of way about Wes Jenkins calling me by my first and last names whenever he approached me. As nice and professional as I was, in my mind I thought Wes was a certified jackass, though I could not and would not ever speak those thoughts out loud to anyone at the campus. Wes was the kind of employee my intuition said I could not trust, but he was also the kind of employee who knew just how far to go without crossing a line for a progressive disciplinary process.

"What do you mean, Wes Jenkins?" My style of petty. Using Wes's first and last name. "First meeting is scheduled at ten."

Wes sipped again.

"Eastern time." Wes handed me a binder with the accreditation team schedule on the front and the report inside. "Didn't you get the updated meeting invite and itinerary over the weekend?"

"What update? I don't know what you're talking about."

"One of their team members had to stay on the East

Coast due to a family emergency, so they're zooming in from D.C. for the opening meeting. But you're late and everyone's waiting to start. Hmm. Not a good look, Taylor James."

"I never got an email, meeting update, or even a text about this."

"Our student assistant was supposed to contact you," Wes said and took another sip from his mug. He feigned a look of confusion. "I don't know what happened."

"I bet you don't. And why would you put Justin Monroe on a task related to the accreditation? You know he's just a junior."

"Hmm. Students can be flakes. Technology these days. Mercury retrograde. A million little things can go wrong. But anyway, don't keep them waiting."

"Don't worry. I won't. I'm ready."

"Oh, I bet you are," Wes said. "By the way, President Weatherspoon is in the conference room with the accreditation team. Waiting, too. You know her schedule is always jam packed."

"But she's got her own solo time on the schedule with the team."

"Schedule change, again. She's flying down to Long Beach later this morning."

"Her chief of staff keeps me updated."

"Somehow, the message came to me."

I wasn't in the mood for Wes's games, and with a room full of people waiting, I knew I had to keep it moving.

"You and I will talk later, Wes Jenkins."

"We will. Good luck with everything, Taylor James."

I was shook by Wes Jenkins, though I wouldn't have admitted that to him. I entered the conference room a nervous wreck. Starting the morning late, keeping the president and the accreditation team waiting—so much for lo-fi beats and the beauty of nature on the morning walk to work centering me. I'd had no chance to make my morning tea, read the report highlights one more time, review the day's agenda again, or make sure that my tie and shirt collar were all right. Wes had definitely unnerved me. Not my style.

Luckily, President Weatherspoon was as supportive and nurturing as she was tough with high standards for excellence. Because the field of higher education was so small, she had known my parents throughout their academic careers. They could call her by her first name, Fiona-Sheree. I called her President Weatherspoon. Despite their professional relationships and camaraderie, I'd made it known through my work that I was not a nepotism baby who'd risen to a vice president's role just because of parental connections. I'd done all the right jobs and planned each of my moves carefully: junior faculty, senior faculty, department chair, dean, and now, vice president for academic affairs and student life.

President Weatherspoon welcomed me into the conference room, wearing a vibrant salmon pink suit with an apple green blouse underneath, and a freshly done braided ponytail with caramel and rose gold highlights sprinkled throughout. For pushing seventy, she stayed looking fly and fashionable. She reminded me a lot of my mother. Surprisingly, the mood was light and airy despite my being late. Coffee, tea, and assorted pastries were on the conference table. Conversation filled the room, the team member who was stuck on the East Coast watching us on Zoom. Nothing like the frantic picture Wes Jenkins had tried to paint minutes earlier.

"Everyone, this is Vice President Dr. Taylor James, the person responsible for leading the accreditation team here at C.U. Lake Merced," said President Weatherspoon, who smiled and led the room in applause. "Dr. James, I was just talking with their team lead here, Dr. Dustin McMillan. I think you two ought to connect about the report before we start."

Again, shook.

I couldn't believe the annoying but incredibly handsome Two Seats Over guy from the other day at Beaux stood before me. In my workplace. Apparently connected with the team evaluating the work I'd done for the university's accreditation process. Eyes on me. Million-dollar smile. Fitted gray suit, matching the same color and style I'd decided to wear that morning. His handshake was firm as President Weatherspoon brought us together and introduced us. Or so she thought. I didn't know how this would go, so I just went with it.

"My pleasure…Dr. Taylor James, is it?"

So, this was the game we were going to play. Pretend like we didn't know each other.

"*Doctor*…? Dustin McMillan."

One more lie of omission added to the heap of lies from a few days earlier. We'd get to that later.

Suddenly, it felt like one of those movies where everyone around us in the room was operating in slow motion, while Dustin and I were in our own little live-action bubble. Our handshake lingered. Our eyes lit up with a little smirk of knowing. He broke the slo-mo scene with that million-dollar smile that had mesmerized me, just a little, the other day at the bar.

"Nice to put faces to names finally," Dustin said, pulling his hand out of mine. "Your work is something."

"Indeed it is," President Weatherspoon said. She paused before stepping away to mingle with some of Dustin's team members. "We're proud of Dr. James. Dr. McMillan, we're impressed with your firm's work. You two are in each other's good hands."

When she was no longer in earshot of us, Dustin closed

in on my ear, mouth within millimeters, and whispered, very sexily and breathlessly, with that baritone, "Good hands, huh?"

"You'll never know."

"Why you standing so close to me?"

"You stepped over to me," I said.

"Because I thought…and think…you fine, Doc."

"We're in a professional setting, D.J., Dustin, Dr. McMillan," I said, putting some space between us. I did not want to initiate any rumors among my colleagues or his for our physical proximity. "You're so full of surprises. What else is there to know?"

I couldn't wait to tell Markell that the drunk and obnoxious stranger from Sunday Funday was the lead consultant on my campus accreditation process. How had we not figured this out prior to this day? After all, we'd been emailing with each other off and on for months.

"I'm an open book. Ask away."

"Ha. You're funny."

"I can be."

"When you're not lying or yelling at your nonbinary cousin."

"We're in a professional setting, Doc," Dustin said, smirking. "We should save that personal part of the convo for later. You ready to get this started, then?"

"Looks like we have no choice. Let's get started."

"You always have a choice, Doc," Dustin said. "And I'm down to start whenever you are."

Such an ass, I thought. An attractive ass, I thought, and I wasn't just referring to how nice his suit pants and jacket bubbled out when he turned and walked away from me.

I cleared my throat to get everyone's attention and started my opening presentation. Though I'd been caught off guard by the early and late meeting start, the hijinks of Wes Jenkins, and the shock of Dustin in my workplace, I got through it all with ease and finesse. I knew the facts, figures, strengths, and weaknesses of California University Lake Merced. I knew the report that I'd compiled thoroughly. Twenty minutes later, I breathed a sigh of relief that I'd finished, without the aid of my script and notes that I'd wanted to use when I thought I had more time to prepare.

I looked around the conference room. President Weatherspoon gave me a thumbs-up and a subtle but supportive smile. I could see positive head nods from the university team I'd assembled for accreditation, and the members of Dustin's team who were assessing our work. Wes Jenkins stood with his arms crossed at the entrance of the conference room door, looking indifferent and unbothered. I could never read what his problem was or why he had one with me. I'd had nothing to do with his being passed over for my job.

Nevertheless, I knew I'd nailed the presentation, though this was only the beginning of many weeks of accreditation work. Confidently, I steepled my hands in front of myself when I'd finished my slides, looked Dustin in his eyes, and asked, "Questions? Comments? Ideas?"

CHAPTER FOUR

Dustin

"With all due respect, Dr. James," I started off as soon as Taylor finished the executive summary presentation for my work team—quite eloquently, I might add, "you presented very well the good work happening at the California University Lake Merced campus. We think your campus's focus on social justice and equity is impeccable. We see the positive impact of many of your initiatives on the campus graduation rates, and we see many examples that illustrate your campus has paid attention to the recommendations another accreditation team made ten years ago."

"Thank you," Taylor said, smiling.

I was loving Taylor's humble confidence and intelligence, which I'd picked up on when we first met at the bar but which came across even more strongly in his presentation. Since the breakup with Silas the go-go dancer, which was strictly about sex, I'd evolved into such a sapiosexual. Quite the evolution from my penchant for athletes and dancers over the years.

"You're welcome, Dr. James," I said, knowing what was coming was going to kill the vibe of Taylor's presentation. "However, this next part I'm going to say surprised us. I've never ever seen a campus accreditation report with so many sections in the wrong format or with data charts and appendices mislabeled. And the typos. It was as if your team sent in a first or second draft to our firm, which I'm sure is not the case."

Leading the university accreditation division of the firm, I worked with universities who contracted us to consult on their internal and external assessment work. Boring as the details sounded to many, I thrived on motivating campus administrators and staff members to do and be better in their work for student success.

Sometimes that meant being tough, sarcastic, offensive, and mean. All in the name of making college campuses better for their constituents. As much as people called me arrogant or egotistical in my evaluations once an accreditation process finished, I knew it was because I did my job well, and sometimes, people didn't expect that level of meticulousness from a Black professional.

"That's so unlike Taylor James," replied Wes, the person who reported to Taylor and who I'd had the most contact with days before arriving to the San Francisco campus. "Can I help and see what's going on? Taylor James and I proofed everything a million times over. Maybe we're slipping. Maybe Taylor James is slipping."

A few giggles peppered the room, but I took control back from Wes, who I sensed was trying to grandstand Taylor in front of his peers. Even in the weeks and days leading up to the visit, I hadn't gotten the best vibes from him. He was one of those higher education people who talked and talked and talked, but nothing they said made sense. And he let professional words slip perilously close to innuendo and intimation of something personal and intimate when I was clearly showing no interest. Through my work, I'd encountered plenty of nice-nasty people working on campuses focused more on game playing with peers than with helping students succeed and graduate.

While I'd had no idea Wes was connected to Taylor via

reporting lines and to the accreditation report process, I knew I needed to make something clear to whomever Wes reported to: Wes was not to be trusted, a ticking time bomb for any student affairs and higher education unit that hired him. And that led me to my next point, which was probably not going to help me with Taylor.

"This report that you submitted is very top heavy and hierarchical," I said matter-of-factly. "What I've read in this *draft* all feels very bureaucratic and procedural, as if there's a disconnect between the work of administration and how it translates on the ground with students. As if there is no team or teamwork here at California University Lake Merced."

"If I may interrupt, Dr. McMillan." Taylor spoke up, his poker face intact with all eyes on him, including President Weatherspoon. "I don't know what report you looked at before coming to campus, but I know we certainly didn't submit a *draft*."

"It reads draft-ish to me," I said, maybe a little too bluntly. "But, hey, instead of going back and forth on this, let me continue with one more point, and then we can adjourn."

"This sounds exactly like the kind of feedback I shared with Taylor James before this report was submitted," Wes said smugly as he pulled out a tablet. "This accreditation is a big deal for us, so I'm just taking notes for the team. Maybe we'll need to remove Taylor James's little student protégé, Justin Monroe, from our project."

I ignored Wes, and I noticed Taylor's face had a look of confusion, embarrassment, and frustration on it. I knew it was time to bring this rocky meeting to an end.

"My final point is this. How much of this report is all reflective of you, Dr. James, instead of it really being a team effort?" I asked. I'd said the same thing at any other place I'd done these accreditation visits, and one person's vision comes through rather than the collective. "I think this teamwork piece is key to the process. Now, I know we've got dozens of interviews with staff, faculty, administration, and students set up for the rest of this week. But I wanted to make sure the weekend retreat piece was still budgeted and planned for."

"It's taken care of already," Wes blurted out, even though I'd aimed the question at Taylor. "I love visiting our sibling campus in Napa Valley. And unlike today, no false starts at the retreat."

President Weatherspoon cut Wes off. "I say we adjourn for now. Dr. James and Dr. McMillan will sidebar. I've got to get to the airport for a flight to Long Beach. We'll circle back and start fresh in the morning. These things happen. Not often, but they happen."

❖

Fifteen minutes later, Taylor and I were face-to-face in his tastefully decorated and compact office a few yards away from the conference room where the disastrous day had begun. He'd turned on a sound diffuser near the office door, which meant that the conversation inside was not to be heard outside the room.

Taylor looked angry. I was nervous both because I didn't know what he was going to say and because it was our first time alone since meeting days before. I remembered how close we'd gotten to kissing at Beaux, or at least how close I was to kissing Taylor, until I'd fucked it up with my cousin. As always, my air of conceit and cockiness was a shield for how excited and giddy I was around any man I'd liked or fallen for.

Before Taylor could begin laying into me, deservedly so, I reached out to give him a conciliatory pat on the arm.

"I apologize, Doc," I said. "We're starting on the wrong foot. Will you accept my apology?"

"No thanks." He pulled away and took off his suit jacket. His soap and cocoa butter scent wafted through the air. He smelled so clean, he ignited my senses, much like the day we met at Beaux. Taylor sat down at his computer desk and stared at the screen, playing with the mouse like he was ignoring me. "This is not going to work. If I'd known you were assigned to work with—"

"'This' as in you and me, Doc? Or 'this' professionally?"

"Both."

"Not fair. How was I supposed to know—"

"Not fair is how you embarrassed me this morning in front of my colleagues and university president. We're old enough to know we don't do that in front of mixed company."

"Do what?"

"Black people embarrassing Black people in front of mixed company. In any setting."

"Doc, we're old enough and professional enough to not be thinking about how we look in front of others."

"We're professional enough and culturally aware enough to give each other a heads-up so we don't have to walk in the room looking unprepared."

"And if I had known it was you, I would have moved heaven and earth to delay this morning's meeting," I said. "It's an unfortunate part of my job. That's why I apologized, Doc."

"Please don't call me Doc anymore. It's annoying. We're both doctors, apparently."

"Hey, how was I to know we would end up working together on your accreditation process? Small gay world. Even smaller higher education world."

"You're smart enough to google or use LinkedIn."

"So are you, Doc."

"Whatever."

"I can't help it that your report was trash."

Taylor turned away from his screen and glared at me. Looked sexy being mad.

"The report I worked on and submitted was not trash," Taylor said. "I personally handled the team, the data collection, the writing, and the submission on the portal. Not that I have to justify or explain to you."

"Well, you kinda do, Doc...I mean Taylor," I said with a chuckle. "I *am* the lead consultant assigned to work with you and your campus. My team and I get to say if your reaccreditation is approved or not."

"It's not gonna work. We can get someone else from Kane-Carlos assigned, I'm sure."

"I'm sure your president won't want to wait another year to get your campus on the calendar," I said. "And by then, your current accreditation will have expired. I don't think you have a choice, unless you want to say you all didn't make your approval because of personality differences."

Taylor turned and fixed his eyes back on his computer screen. "Fine. Whatever." He paused, then a beat later said, "Just because I wouldn't give you the time of day at Beaux."

"Ahh, we're getting somewhere, Doc...Taylor," I said. "This, today, is professional. That, the other day, is personal. We can fix both."

"Nothing to fix," Taylor said. "Work is work. Personally, your life sounds like a mess I don't want to get mixed up in."

"I think you're so..." I started to say "cute" but remembered that this was still Taylor's work setting, and we were on an assignment together, and I still had a lot of explaining to do about my multiple names and aliases, family issues, roots in the Bay Area, and the ex-factor who really wasn't a factor except for the refrigerator deal. Besides, cute wasn't a word men in their forties called other men in their forties, even if the Black wasn't cracked. "If it's not stepping across a line. I like it when you're not nice, Taylor. Not-nice Taylor seems like a real Taylor. The kind of Taylor I like. If he'd give this a chance."

"Again, no 'this,'" Taylor said, air quoted, and then continued scrolling on his screen as if I wasn't in the room with him. "Anyway, so are you D.J.? Junior? Dustin? Dr. McMillan? You're a man of many identities. I don't know who I'm talking to or what you're trying to hide with all these names. I guess I could google you now and ask questions later."

"Or you could just break down and get to know me. I'm here in front of you. Now. If you want."

Why was I working so hard to get Dr. Taylor James when he obviously didn't want to be gotten—as a fuck buddy, a potential date, or anything else? And who was I to think being enamored with someone I met randomly in a Castro neighborhood bar could turn into something when I could link up with so many back home? Especially when I was heading back to Chicago in four or five weeks once this San Francisco assignment was done. Plenty of Black men there. Plenty of men there, period, who wanted me. I knew my worth and value. Maybe Taylor was right. It was not going to work, personally or professionally, for us.

After no response from Taylor about getting to know me, I said, "Fine. Have it your way. If you can get this contract changed, nice. It's been good knowing you. And I'll get you your money you gave to Manessa. I hope you find whatever it is you need or want, Doc."

Taylor huffed and looked up from his computer again. "Maybe we should exchange numbers," he said, taking out his phone. "I mean, in case I can't get someone else assigned from your company, and we do have to work on this project together."

"We'll see what happens, I guess." I took my phone out and let it hover over his for our contact information to transmit. "Maybe we can grab a meal and discuss the project? Or work on the project and have food delivered? Lots to clean up and clear up after your presentation this morning."

Taylor gave me a deadpan gaze. I lowkey liked making him mad. "Just so you're clear, this doesn't mean anything, D.J., Junior, Dustin. However you want to be called. This is work. Strictly work."

CHAPTER FIVE

Taylor

"So, I guess you're stuck with me, huh, Doc?" Dustin said after he slid his overnight bag into the back seat of the Prius I was borrowing from the university. His color-coordinated light gray sweatshirt, sweatpants, and Timberland boots matched the gloomy Friday morning weather. He smiled and continued, his voice with a hint of playfulness, as his delicious scent floated into the car. "I promise, I'm a good copilot."

After a week of committee meetings and what seemed like endless inquiries and interviews about life at California University Lake Merced, we were departing for a partial weekend team retreat Dustin insisted was an important part of the accreditation process.

I'd done everything I could since that disastrous first work meeting to get out of the contract with the Kane-Carlos Collective. Impossible. From my mom's guilt-tripping me that "Jameses don't quit," to President Weatherspoon giving me a directive to continue the accreditation process as is, I had no choice but to move on with it.

I loved my current job as a university vice president, after all. I aspired to be a campus president for my next job. Getting through a successful reaccreditation process would set me up to be a strong presidential candidate. Realistically, I'd known the process wasn't going to stop, but as someone who'd had a pretty easy life without much resistance, I thought I'd at least try. Needless to say, I was stuck working with Dustin on this project for at least another few weeks. I couldn't wait for it to be done—the accreditation and the ride together to the retreat site, our sister California University campus in Napa Valley.

"We'll see about that," I said, annoyed, and rolled my eyes, which Dustin could not see as he got into the front passenger seat and clicked the seat belt. I still needed to be nice and cordial with Dustin since his final word would determine if our campus received a passing grade or not. "But just so you know, I'm not big on talking and driving at the same time. Nothing personal."

"All right with me," he said. "I mean, we're just stuck in the car together for like an hour and a half."

"You volunteered to ride with me," I said. "You could have jumped on the sprinter van to Napa with everyone else."

"I get carsick on buses."

"But not in compact cars like this?"

"Not with good company like you, Doc," Dustin said, smiling. "You're stuck with me. Ready to take me on a good ride?"

Dustin's innuendo and teasing were kinda cute. But even though we would be stuck together for the short drive to Napa and the longer accreditation process, I wasn't going to let him distract me.

"What'd I say about calling me Doc?"

"Point taken."

"Anyway, it'll be just enough time for finishing up a podcast or an Audible," I said, ignoring his efforts to flirt. "Hope you don't mind listening to the *Bad Queers* or *Minoritea Report* podcast."

"Fine with me," he said, reaching down into the backpack on the floor between his feet. "I'll read this new book I picked up at Fabulosa Books. Or I'll put on my headphones. Something about Beyoncé's *Renaissance* gets me in a good mood. You don't know anything about that, hmm? Being in a good mood?"

Dustin and I stared at each other. I wanted to crack a smile, as he always seemed to have something to say to get a rise out of me, but I didn't.

"Ooh. Smart, Dustin," I said. "I get it. I remember how we met."

"Do you?"

"I'm not stupid," I said, pressing the ignition button to get us started on our journey. "Let's go. Lunch and wine tasting at one, right? Don't wanna be late for the 'bonding' start of the retreat."

"Don't be so pressed about it. It's for *your* team's good."

"We get along fine," I said.

"Do we?"

"Anyway, Dustin, don't know what kind of copilot you're gonna be with your headphones on."

"Oh, so you do wanna talk then, Doc—I mean, Taylor? It's gonna slip sometime."

"Whatever works for you."

"I mean better me here riding with you than Wes Jenkins."

Out of the corner of my right eye, I could see Dustin looking at me from the passenger seat. I tried to keep my reaction inside, but I couldn't help but laugh. Dustin laughed, too.

"I'm just saying."

"You said it, not me."

"I'm not trying to throw shade or anything, and I know

you and I gotta keep it professional," Dustin said. "But that Wes Jenkins is one of those ambitious queens you gotta watch out for. He's something."

"Indeed, he is," I said, knowing Dustin was truth telling, but also aware he and I were only connected by his temporary contract job, and I wouldn't throw a colleague under the bus even if Wes Jenkins and I weren't the closest. "My bestie Markell thinks—well, says the same thing. Said Wes Jenkins is always so extra with the staff when he's at Beaux and leaves like two-dollar tips when Markell gives him comps and discounts at the bar all night."

"Hmm, another frugal tipper," Dustin said. "Sounds familiar."

"Whatever."

"I remember how we met, Doc."

I rolled my eyes. "Why are you like this?"

"Like what?"

"Never mind. Forget it."

"We're forever connected by *Renaissance*, you can't deny it," Dustin said, laughing. "Where'd you see the concert?"

"Labor Day weekend in L.A. on her birthday night. And on the Saturday night before. You?"

"Look at you, fancy," Dustin said. "Me. Chicago in the summer. And Paris. Memorial Day weekend. Blue Ivy's first performance."

"Lucky you. And fancy back."

"I have good taste." Dustin thumped my hand, which was sitting on the center console in between us. I saw that Chopard watch on his wrist and knew his taste and spending were one thing he was honest about. "In lots of things."

"That watch says it all."

"Oh, you watching, huh?" he asked. "No pun intended. You get it?"

"You're so corny."

About twenty minutes later, we'd made our way from campus through the rush hour traffic heading north on Nineteenth Avenue. We'd emerged from the winding roads and lush greenery of Golden Gate Park, and in the distance could see the Golden Gate Bridge. Farther away on the horizon, sunshine. Weather was consistently sunnier and warmer minutes away from campus and outside the San Francisco city limits.

"Can I ask you a favor, Doc, I mean Taylor?"

"Whatever, call me what you will," I said. "What's that?"

"Before we cross the bridge, can we make a stop?"

"You gotta use it already?"

"Nothing like that," Dustin said. "But it would mean a lot to me. I promise we won't be late to lunch and wine tasting."

I let Dustin reset the navigation, and a few minutes later, I was pulling into a parking spot at Crissy Field, a national park site I'd heard of but had never been to in the years I'd lived in San Francisco.

"Oh my," I said, in awe of the stunning views of the Golden Gate Bridge, the San Francisco Bay, and downtown San Francisco. "This is amazing."

"It really is," Dustin said, looking at me. "Thank you for stopping. You're too kind."

"I mean, we do have a little bit of time before we have to be in Napa."

"Then don't waste time. Let's get out and walk a bit."

I marveled at the activity in the space on a random Friday morning—people windsurfing in the choppy waters of San Francisco Bay, kiteboarding and skateboarding and biking on the promenade, playing with their unleashed dogs in the open, green fields of grass, and walking and running along the waterfront paths, where Dustin and I strolled slowly while enjoying the beauty of nature on the northern tip of San Francisco.

"For someone who talked so much mess about San Francisco when we first met, you've redeemed yourself with this, Dustin."

"Where was the lie, though?" Dustin threw his hands up in front of him. I couldn't help but notice how his arms flexed against the sleeves of his gray sweatshirt. Looked like a solid set of biceps hiding there. Looked like a solid set of everything hiding underneath the sweatpants, firm and solid like in his tight suits he pranced around work in.

"I'm trying to be nice. To give you a compliment."

"Aww, thank you," Dustin said. "You are nice. Too nice to me. Especially coming across like the asshole I can be at the bar the other day. And at work this week."

"Yeah, you were and *are* a lot," I said, giving gave him a playful pat on the shoulder. Solid shoulders, too, I noticed. "It's giving defensiveness. It's giving trying to be tough but probably not. It's definitely giving insecurely secure."

"You're giving psychiatrist, Doc. In fact, giving TV psychiatrist like that Dr. Taylor Hayes shrink on *Bold and the Beautiful*. I used to watch it back in the day with my ma. Saint Taylor, they called her. I still watch now, that and *Young and the Restless*, when I get a chance."

"Oh wow, that's funny. I get pinged online every now and then by soap opera fans, just because my name is Dr. Taylor James," I said. "I'm a pretty good person, I've been told. But I'm no saint."

"Can't get to be our age and not done some good and bad things—with some good and not-so-good people."

"Like your ex, Silas?" I asked. "I mean, not that I'm trying to get in your business or anything."

"It's no big deal, Doc," Dustin said. "What's that cliché

about people, reasons, and seasons? Anyway, that reminds me to get you back your money for that situation with my cousin Manessa and the fridge deal with my ma. I ain't forgot. And thanks."

We looked at each other and smiled. I didn't want to make a deal out of his family dynamics unless he wanted to go there. We continued along the parkway. It felt easy, walking, talking, and being with Dustin in a casual, non-work environment.

"This whole scene is giving life, money, freedom," I said while looking at the casual busyness around us. There was a gentle breeze coming off the bay, and the sun was beginning to break through. "I mean, do these people work?"

"Ha."

"And we're the only two Black people within eyeshot. Two Black men with doctorates casually strolling like nothing. On a Friday morning. It's so weird."

"I only know about this place because we used to come here for field trips all the way from Oakland when we were kids," Dustin said. "Part of this gifted and talented program for students at so-called at-risk schools."

"As in underfunded or unfunded."

"Right," Dustin said. "And since I don't get out this way much anymore, I…I really appreciate you taking the detour. I hope you like it."

"What have I been missing in my almost five years living here? This is amazing, Dustin. A-maz-ing." I elongated the word a while because the area truly was amazing and beautiful and just five miles away from campus and my apartment.

"And all it took was me for you to find it," he said. "Maybe I'm the missing piece."

"We're not going there," I said, smiling. "This is work. Only work."

"Let's call it a work date, then."

"I don't date," I said. "I work. I stay focused. I want to be a college president one day."

"You may not know this, Doc," Dustin said. "But I make college presidents. The Kane-Carlos Collective makes presidents."

"What do you mean?"

"I've done quite a few of these accreditations and program reviews for campuses since I joined the firm a few years ago," he said. I listened intently. "In each one, the person or persons who led the process on their campus eventually got some type of promotion. Or eventually became a president of a campus somewhere else. But you're smart, allegedly. I'm sure you took this project on with your ambitions in mind."

"I'm not calculating like that. I'm not a Wes Jenkins," I said, laughing. Dustin laughed, too. "And I was voluntold to do this. What President Weatherspoon asks, I do."

"I can tell that the grand diva, Dr. Fiona-Sheree Weatherspoon, likes and respects you. Your team, too." Dustin paused. "Me, too."

"Stop. Stop. Stop." I was flattered, yet I didn't want to give any false messages that our connection would evolve beyond being professional colleagues.

"All right," Dustin said, putting his hands up. "Fine. I'll stop. I see I made you smile, though."

"That you did. Thanks."

"I'll hit you up about us in a couple years when you become President Taylor James."

"Is that your way of saying that we're getting reaccredited?"

"Not at all. I mean, we still have the weekend retreat and a couple more weeks of work together."

"Right."

"If I do well on this project with you, I think I'll be up for a senior partner role in the Kane-Carlos Collective. No, I *know*

I'll be up for a promotion if your team gives positive feedback about the work I'm doing with you all."

"So, you better stay on your best behavior, Dustin, if you want that promotion."

I smiled and winked at Dustin.

"Then you better get your campus reaccredited, if you want to be a college president."

He smiled and winked back at me.

We continued walking, mostly in silence as we took in more scenery and activity around us, until we reached Crissy Field Beach East, which offered us a beautiful postcard view of both the beach and the Golden Gate Bridge. A few photographers and their clients lined parts of the beach, all aiming for a perfect shot.

"Are you two a couple?" a nearby voice called out to us. I'd heard that line before on one of those meet-cute social media sites that I followed. "Want me to take your picture?"

"Oh no," Dustin and I both said at the same time, laughing.

"Brothers?"

We started up again. "We work—"

"Well, you two look like you're more than friends. I can still take your picture, though."

After a couple of solo and duo shots with our phones, we thanked the random photographer and marveled at all the pictures taken of us with the majestic Golden Gate Bridge positioned perfectly behind us. The detour was worth it. We'd both come away with dozens of new photos for posting on our socials at some point—Dustin in his gray sweats and Timberlands, me in a black turtleneck and black jeans. I'd enjoyed being a tourist with Dustin for a few minutes on this almost perfect spring day.

"Thanks for a beautiful morning, Dustin," I said as we returned to the parking lot and the campus car. I looked at my watch, one not nearly as fancy and expensive as the Chopard Dustin wore. "We still have time to make it to Napa Valley in time for lunch and afternoon wine tasting—and the oh-so-exciting bonding exercises."

"I don't know about that, Doc," Dustin said, pointing to the passenger side of the car. The window had been shattered, glass sprinkled on the parking lot pavement, and the back passenger door was wide open. "Looks like we been got. A smash-and-grab. Fuck."

"Oh no. Anything missing?"

I pressed the fob to open the trunk. My luggage was still there. Dustin looked in the front and back seats where he'd put his overnight bag and backpack.

"All my shit's gone," Dustin said. "Man, these fuckers work fast. And in broad fucking daylight."

We sat side by side on the curb near the car and decided to split the follow-up duties. Dustin called the team riding on the sprinter van to let them know what had happened and asked one of his teammates to continue the day one itinerary as planned until we arrived. I called the captain of the campus safety department first for guidance on dealing with the university car, campus insurance, and with the city's police, since we were off campus.

As we waited, I looked over at Dustin, who appeared defeated and sad.

"We got this, Dustin," I said, trying to provide some assurance. "We're in this together. We'll be okay."

CHAPTER SIX

Dustin

The car break-in situation took me back to a space I thought I'd escaped by leaving Oakland and my family behind. A space where you were open to losing your things and money. A space where you had to fight family, neighbors, and strangers from taking what's yours. A space where life was about day-to-day survival.

Because of dealing with the police, making statements for the report, and waiting on a new campus car to be delivered to us, Taylor and I were late to Napa. We missed lunch and wine tasting with the group. We missed a quick session on strategic planning. We missed the "deep questions" session I was to have facilitated during dinner and just before the group headed out to an evening jazz music performance.

We'd also missed the prime housing and roommate assignments to the two-bedroom, two-bath cottages. Taylor and I were put together in a leftover loft house no one else wanted to be assigned to—the one with a bedroom upstairs that overlooked the downstairs living room with a pullout sofa and no walls except the one bathroom and a couple of closets. It was definitely giving the vibes of an HGTV open floor plan renovation, especially for a household that didn't want or need alone space.

"So much for privacy," I said, looking around as we entered our sleeping quarters. At least one good thing came out of the theft. Though we were in Napa Valley for work, I was feeling extreme excitement and butterflies knowing I'd get to share a space with Taylor. "I guess we're really going to bond during the retreat."

Taylor sat his luggage next to the sofa in the living room and looked around. I sat my shopping bags and newly purchased duffel bag on the sofa. Before arriving at the campus, Taylor was kind enough to take me to a nearby outlet mall close to Napa where I could purchase a pair of pants, couple of shirts, underwear, workout clothes for the ropes course, something to sleep in, and toiletries—all the things I needed to replace immediately. A laptop and tablet were already on order with the Kane-Carlos Collective, as we were confident that even with AirTags, we wouldn't get ours back.

"It's quaint, that's for sure," Taylor said as he looked up, where, from the living room, we could see the upstairs bedroom. "Definitely no privacy. We'll make the most of it. You want up or down?"

"Doesn't matter," I said, reading a note sitting in front of a basket on the nearby kitchen counter. "Looks like we've got dinner and sparkly in the fridge. And wine and chocolate and all sorts of goodies in the basket. I see you, Cal U Napa Valley."

"Let's just say they got money. They are one of the more well-resourced Cal U campuses, not just because of the old-school wealth and donors living up here in Napa but also because of their academic programs in viticulture, enology, business, and other related majors. And these dorms, I mean residence halls—fancy."

"In other words, privileged campus for privileged

people," I said, walking to the rear part of the living room. "Some people just have it so easy."

"Fortunately, and unfortunately."

Curious and intrigued, I slid open the patio door just off the living room. A golden, radiant sunset illuminated the rolling hills and vineyards.

"Look at this, Taylor." I gestured for him to come out to the deck. "Gorgeous."

We stood in silence for a few minutes taking in the sunset.

"Twice in one day, Dustin."

"What's that?"

"That we're experiencing the beauty of nature together."

I saw Taylor glance at me out the corner of my eye. I turned to look at him, and our eyes locked. If this had been one of those romance channel movies, this would have been a perfect moment to go in for a kiss. It had only been a few days, but I felt like I'd made my intentions known. Taylor was hard to read. Was there interest? Had I come on too quick and too strong? Could there be a possibility? Only one way to find out.

"Twice in one day," I said, eyes still fixed on Taylor and his on mine. "Lucky. Except for that break-in. But I won't let that break the mood."

"I'm sorry that happened and that your things were stolen," Taylor said. "You okay? You good?"

"I'm okay," I said, laughing. "Except that outlet mall ain't have no Lululemon, North Face, Patagonia, or other name brands I'd buy."

"Dustin, really? We are alive and you have what you need."

"I know. I know. I know. You did me a solid taking me shopping for the basics. It's not designer, but it'll do."

"The brands mean that much to you?"

"You're sounding judgey," I said. "I'm not trying to get deep or anything with you, but the break-in incident, though. I thought I'd escaped that part of my life. Kinda made me think of some of my growing up years. Things I don't like to remember or think about."

"I get it. And I don't. Whatever you want to share or not share. It's all right with me, Dustin."

"First, give me your app to pay you back right now." I grabbed Taylor's hand with his phone in it. I pulled mine out from my pocket with my free hand. Touching Taylor's soft skin felt electric, even though it was just to get a task done that had been nagging on my mind for the past week or so. I put my phone on top of his, information and money transferred, and we put our phones away. "Thank you. And now that that's out of the way, what was your question again?"

"Are you okay, Dustin? With what happened earlier today?"

"You grow up used to things getting broken into, stolen, left, abandoned, borrowed and never paid back, taken advantage of, used, being called only when people want something, all that, you feel me?" I said. I couldn't believe I was unloading like that on Taylor. But he asked and he continued looking at me the entire time. Such a psychiatrist. "It feels like a violation, of course, but at least now I have the means to replace things that get stolen or taken from me. It's a feeling I don't like, but hey, it happened. Moving on. Thanks for asking. For listening."

"Of course. Thanks for sharing."

"You're too kind, Taylor," I said. "I want to apologize, again, for the shaky start, omitting so much about my life and being a basic asshole."

"We're all human. You don't owe me anything, let alone an apology. People make mistakes or show you who they are."

"Thank you," I said. My heart was beating in overdrive sharing and opening up to Taylor. I knew it was work that had brought us together, but this moment on the patio with the sunset upon us magnified the feelings I had for Taylor. "I don't know why you're so kind to me."

"What makes you think you don't deserve kindness, Dustin?"

"I never thought of it like that."

And I hadn't. I was intrigued and confused. Taylor was making me think about myself.

"Well," Taylor said. He broke the gaze and began walking back inside the cottage. How could he just stop a moment of intimacy like that? Right when I was opening up to him and telling him things I didn't even want to think about or admit to myself. How dare he? I followed like a puppy dog to the kitchen. "We should heat up our dinner," he said. "Open up a bottle. Take in this sunset before it disappears."

"All right," I said, a little confused about the sudden shift in energy as we both made our way around the tiny kitchen. I hoped my mini disclosure hadn't turned Taylor off or turned him away from wanting to know me more. I hoped I hadn't gotten too deep, or my story seemed too pitiful.

Dinner was warmed and plated, and the wine uncorked and poured. Samara Joy on speaker for background music. We returned to the deck to enjoy the sunset again before the warmth of the evening gave over to the chilly nighttime air.

I was still a bit put off Taylor had changed the subject so abruptly when I shared what I'd shared with him. No reflection back. No commentary. No acknowledgment, really. Just a flip question and remark to me. I made a mental note but decided not to make a deal of it and kept the mood light.

"This is delicious. What you think?" I asked Taylor, as we started eating the dinner left behind for us—grilled chicken breast strips with that hint of smoke embedded in the meat, a side of pasta shells with seasoned vegetables and a lemony sauce, and half a roasted sweet potato.

"That this is perfection," he said. "The food, the scenery, the wine, the music, the relaxation. Cheers."

We clinked our glasses of Chardonnay, smiled, nodded, and took healthy sips.

"One and done for us," I said. "And I'm not talking one bottle. We have ropes course in the morning after an early breakfast."

"Oh, joy." Taylor rolled his eyes and assembled a forkful of pasta. "Team building. Facilitated by you."

"By yours truly."

"Maybe you can facilitate a 'deep questions' conversation for the two of us to pass the time while we're eating," he said. "Show me what I would have experienced earlier. Show me how you earn your money with the Kane-Carlos Collective."

We smiled and laughed.

"I'll only do two, since we need to clean up, pick a bed, and get some sleep," I said. "You been putting me through it today."

"Whatever, Dustin." I loved Taylor's nerdy-sounding "whatever," emphasis on the final "er" whenever he said it.

"So, here's the first question I would have asked pairs to answer with each other," I said. "Why are you doing the work you do in higher education? You do this one. We both can answer the next."

"Good question, and it's simple. To me, higher education is the greatest tool of social change that moves people upward. Earning a degree or achieving the next one gives people a life of choice and agency, in my opinion," Taylor said, sounding like a pageant contestant or something. Like he just knew his life and purpose. "I guess I never really thought of it before. It's all

I've seen and known, given that I'm like the third generation of educators. I like being part of that change in people's lives by being in this field. So many of my former students are doing great things with their lives because of earning their degrees. Yet, there's a misinformation movement trying to shake our confidence in higher education. Next to a higher power and family, there's nothing like higher education. To me, anyway."

"Oh yeah, the book bans and politicians going after college presidents, right," I said. "Must be nice coming from a family of educators. Wanna tell me more?"

"I could talk all day about my family and education. But here's the CliffsNotes or Too Long; Didn't Read version," Taylor said, laughing. "My people moved out to California generations ago from Louisiana and Texas. Everyone became some kind of a teacher or advocate. I grew up in the Ladera Heights area in L.A. Grew up around Black educators, doctors, attorneys, and politicians. My parents are academics and administrators at the Cal U East L.A. campus. I've been in college all my life basically."

"I see. Must be nice."

"It's just my life. I mean, I'm lucky to have the parents I have, and to have the adopted brother I have in Markell. I don't know. We've traveled everywhere. We volunteer. We donate and give back to the community. I've had an easy life, I guess you could say."

"So y'all Jameses were some modern-day Huxtables," I said, and then I regretted it, equating Taylor's family life to that of a TV sitcom family. I didn't intend to project anything that came across as judgmental, though in a way, I was. I didn't know if it was judgmental or jealousy of the way Taylor grew up, and so I tried to clean it up. "Not that there's anything wrong with that. You're lucky. Not every Black person gets to grow up like you. You don't know what it's like when your mom chooses men and money over you. I'm talking too much. Sorry."

"Want to unpack anything about what you just said?"

"Nah. Not now. I've said too much."

"We can go back to that anytime," Taylor said, not reacting or flinching like some people would when disclosing too much too soon. "So what's the next deep question?"

Awkwardly, I kept it moving.

"For both of us," I said, still shook at how quickly Taylor could change topics with no emotion. "What were our first impressions of each other? I can go first since you just talked for such a long time already."

"The shade, Dustin."

I paused for a second and looked Taylor in the eyes.

"I thought you were the most handsome man in Beaux that afternoon. I was mesmerized and knew I had to get to know you. That's why I sat down by you and probably got on your nerves. I thought you smelled good, whatever that soap and lotion you use are. I was impressed by your generosity, not just with my cousin Manessa, but with the other performers apparently. I thought, at the time, you were attentive and a good listener."

"At the time?"

"I'm still feeling that one out," I said, thinking about how Taylor just up and changed the subject on me a few minutes earlier. "I'll leave it at that for now, Doc. What about you of me? First impression?"

"I had none," Taylor said, looking at me. "Okay. First impression. I thought you were cocky, conceited, and definitely confident. Cute. Like the kind of guy who knows what and who he wants and is used to getting what and who he wants."

"What? Me? My rizz came across as cocky? No way."

"Yes way," Taylor said, sipping on his wine. "And what's

with the Gen-Z slang, millennial? Rizz, for real? Anyway. The question was about first impressions. I also thought you were a bit of a…not quite liar, but not quite truth teller."

"Man, I'm hurt." I smiled, but I understood where that came from. "Go on."

"That's all. I answered your question."

We paused and stared at each other.

"That was your first impression, Doc," I said. "What about now?"

I saw a hint of a smile Taylor tried to suppress, our eyes still meeting.

"I think first impressions can be not totally accurate," Taylor said. "I think you are…"

Just as Taylor was telling me what he thought of me, the doorbell to our cottage rang and in walked Wes Jenkins without a greeting or invitation.

"What are you doing here, Wes Jenkins?" Taylor asked as Wes walked through the cabin like he owned it and came out to the back patio where we were sitting. His white polo shirt and khakis looked straight out of the catalog of Carlton Banks from *Fresh Prince of Bel-Air*.

"What's going on here, Taylor James—and Dustin McMillan?" Wes asked and looked around the patio at our half-eaten dinner plates and almost empty wine glasses. "Looks like a date night or something."

"Nothing like that, Wes Jenkins," Taylor said. "The 'deep questions' session. Dustin wanted me to see what I missed."

"We were late for everything, so Taylor and I just decided to chill and rest up before tomorrow morning's ropes course."

"Hmm, I see," Wes said. "If that's what you say. I mean, our respective teams did come up here to bond, but if our leaders can't even join us to—"

"What do you want, Wes Jenkins?" Taylor asked. I liked

the feisty in Taylor as much as I disliked the obnoxious in Wes. "You already know what kind of day Dustin and I have had and why we were late. I mean, technology. It works. We called and informed. So, what's up?"

"Excuse me for seeing a few lights on in your place and wanting to inform you," Wes said, "that a couple people are gonna have to sit out tomorrow morning due to food poisoning and stomach issues. Hopefully no one else, since we all have been eating at the same dining facilities and wineries."

Taylor and I looked at our half-eaten plates and our eyes widened.

I let an "ewww" escape from my mouth and Wes continued. "But I'm sure everything will be okay with you two. Just wanted to update you."

"Thanks, Wes Jenkins. I appreciate that."

Wes continued looking around the patio and made his way back into the cottage. He looked at our luggage and bags, still packed, on and near the sofa.

"I think there's another bed upstairs in the loft," Wes said. He pointed at the bags and then upstairs. "This is a work retreat, Taylor James. We are in the middle of an accreditation process being led by Dustin. I know you two wouldn't do anything to make it seem like there was anything going on to put our process up for ethics questions."

"We haven't unpacked yet, Wes," I said. "We barely had time for dinner."

"And wine. And ambience music. And what looked like intimate conversation on the patio when I walked in."

"I don't know what you're implying, Wes Jenkins," Taylor said, incensed at what Wes was saying, as if we were children or reported to him. "But you and I both know how important it is for the university accreditation to go successfully. None of us will jeopardize that."

Wes was silent. Kept looking from Taylor to me, me to Taylor.

"If you say so," Wes said. "Just remember, I don't want the integrity of this process tainted. It's important for all of us that everything is on the up-and-up. It's work. It's professional. Nothing personal. We hired your firm, Dustin. Your job is on the line, too."

I didn't know where Wes's accusations were coming from. Certainly, Taylor and I hadn't given any hints of anything beyond a professional relationship, mostly because there was nothing beyond a professional relationship. It was all by chance we'd driven together, gotten delayed, and been randomly selected to be roommates because we were late. Yes, we'd shared some personal conversations, much like the rest of the group had been doing during the first day of retreat.

"I definitely know all of our jobs are on the line," I said. "Nothing to worry about in terms of crossing any boundaries. It's just work. Right?"

Wes exited, and we watched him walk down the path where their student assistant, Justin Monroe, was standing and waiting. Wes's visit had definitely killed any vibe Taylor and I were kinda creating that evening.

I thought that even with any feelings I was developing for Taylor, I wouldn't and couldn't cross any line that made the accreditation process seem like it was based on anything personal.

"So, Wes Jenkins knows how to chill a mood," Taylor said as he let out a little yawn. "I've got to spend more time with Justin, to make sure he doesn't turn out cynical and jaded like Wes. I promised Justin's dad I'd look out for his son when he enrolled at CU Lake Merced."

"I don't know how you do it, putting up with Wes at work," I said. "And yeah, keep Wes away from influencing students."

"Occupational hazard, I guess. Anyway. It's getting late. Time to decide who wants upstairs and who wants here?"

"I'll take the upstairs loft," I said, picking up my shopping bags and heading toward the stairs. "Not a problem."

A few seconds later, I headed down the stairs with my shopping bags and sat them next to my newly purchased duffel bag.

"What happened?" Taylor asked.

"So much for staying upstairs. There is no bed. No linens. No sheets. No pallet. Nothing."

"What? Are you for real?"

"Check for yourself. Looks like we are sharing the pullout sofa."

"No way," Taylor said, rolling his eyes. "This isn't what I had in mind for this retreat bonding weekend. Sleeping in the same bed is a little too much togetherness for me."

"Same," I said. "Not in my plan either. But we need to get some rest. So, back to your question."

"The question of…?"

"You want the left side or the right side of the bed?"

CHAPTER SEVEN

Taylor

I woke up just before the alarm was set to go off at six. But just before the alarm, I was dreaming of singing birds, cool breezes, and a warm body pressing into mine.

I opened my eyes quickly and began assessing the morning scene. Napa. Sofa bed. Living room. My back was turned to Dustin, and one of his arms and a leg were draped over me. Our hot, moist skin stuck against each other under the covers. I didn't know how long we'd spent sleeping in the little spoon and big spoon position, or how we ended up that way during the night, but it wasn't what I'd planned when we discovered there was only one bed in our cottage and no other options were available. I thought about that Deborah Cox song "Nobody's Supposed to Be Here" because Dustin and I weren't supposed to end up like this. I tried to gently disentangle from him.

"Don't go yet," Dustin said in an even more groggy baritone voice, his face nestled comfortably between my neck and shoulder. I could smell his morning breath and the subtle aroma that he needed to brush his teeth and take a shower. Dustin squeezed and pulled me closer, definitely rigid and excited behind me as he pressed into my butt. "Can I get some, babe? We can take our time, Silas. It's the weekend."

He was in the middle of a morning dream, too.

Feeling Dustin's morning arousal was hot, but I couldn't lie there and pretend to be his ex. That was not consensual. Definitely not in our plan to keep our connection strictly professional either. What if Wes Jenkins or another colleague walked in unexpectedly for an in-person wake-up call? I gathered strength and rolled out of his hold, standing up beside the sofa bed.

"Dustin, it's me," I whispered, looked down at him, and tapped him on the shoulder to wake him gently. "It's Taylor, not Silas."

Dustin opened his eyes slowly and looked around, like he was coming out of a fog. His eyes opened wider, quickly, once he realized I was there and where we were.

"Shit," Dustin said, looking down at his erection hanging out of the bottom of his boxer briefs. He pulled the covers back over his legs. "I dreamed I was fucking my ex. I'm sorry. This is so inappropriate. I'm embarrassed. It felt so good, so real."

I didn't know if I should gasp at seeing Dustin's dick, which was impressive, or giggle at his embarrassment.

"You definitely called out his name," I said, trying to keep thoughts of Dustin sexing his ex, whom I'd only heard about, out of my head. "Silas must be on your mind, based on what I felt, you did, and I just saw."

"Oh my. I'm so sorry, Taylor. I would never call you another guy's name. We're not even supposed to be…like this. I would never touch you like that without consent. I hope you know that."

Dustin pointed at me standing over him in my boxer briefs and tank top and him in his boxer briefs, thin sheet covering his dick print, and no tank top. Then I noticed the elaborate ink work on his chiseled arms, chest, and abs—abs that transitioned into a "V" right above his underwear line. Tattoos and Black skin had come a long way, academic me thought while taking in all of Dustin. This isn't your granddad's forties, superficial me thought while unexpectedly eyeing Dustin's body. Practical me thought we probably shouldn't have gone to bed with next to nothing on, knowing we'd be sharing a sofa bed, but, as we'd discussed, it was how we slept when we were at our own places.

"You don't have to apologize or explain, Dustin. But I'll accept it. I believe you."

Dustin turned over and grabbed his watch, which was sitting on the arm of the sofa.

"Fuck," he said. "Sorry for cussing so much. I can't believe… We need to get ready for the ropes course."

"It's all good," I said, smiling. I turned away so he could adjust himself or let himself deflate. "I can give you some extra time in the bathroom this morning. I'll put on some music, turn up the TV, or take a walk outside if you need to take care of yourself."

"I can't jack off knowing you're sitting here in the living room or kitchen. Knowing you're so close when I'm getting close."

"You're not supposed to be thinking of me that way anyway, Dustin," I said as I walked to the kitchen. "I'll make some smoothies with whatever is in the fridge while you shower."

"Thanks, Taylor. I did not mean to call you Silas."

I wasn't a jealous type. But I did wonder what hold Silas had over Dustin's mind, memory, and senses.

❖

It was just before noon, and the afternoon heat was starting to trickle into the valley. We'd just finished the morning ropes course Dustin facilitated for our teams, and I was a hot, sweaty, exhausted mess. Lucky for us all, we'd be packing, loading up, and driving back to the cool weather of San Francisco in a couple hours. The retreat weekend—well, the day and a half—was winding down quickly.

"I actually enjoyed myself this morning, Dustin," I said softly as we walked back slowly to the cottage we were sharing. The crunch of the gravel beneath our feet punctuated the silence, as most of the team walked ahead or behind us quietly, fatigued from the morning experience together. "And no food poisoning. Thank you."

"That would have made for a not-so-fun sleeping arrangement," Dustin said. "Stomach gurgles and sleeping in the same bed. Especially with me all pressed up against you like I was this morning."

"No bueno," I said. "Let's just forget about it. It's never going to happen again. I don't really care how your ex is on your mind." I kinda did want to know more about Dustin and Silas, but that really wasn't my business.

"Don't worry, he's not."

"If you say so, Dustin."

"Jealous?"

"Not at all," I said. "Let's change the subject."

"Wait. How about let's get back to what you just said, though, before the Silas talk. Kind words from you, Doc? What is the world coming to?"

"These ropes courses are not my thing, not gonna lie," I said. "I never understood why so many people in higher education like to do them. But it looks like it did the job. There was bonding. And now everyone is ready to knock out on the ride home."

"Hold on, Doc," Dustin said to me, interrupting our

conversation to shout out to our teammates who were beginning to disappear from the gravel path into their cottages. "You all got a little over an hour to shower, pack, and be on the van. Box lunches will be waiting for you."

His take-charge voice and command of the group made me start to look at Dustin in a different light. He had confidence listening to, interpreting, and mirroring back team members' reactions to the exercises while facilitating discussion, and he was convinced this weekend retreat would do wonders for my university team, his team, and ultimately the accreditation process. All morning, I was trying to concentrate on being present and in the moment. At the same time, I was feeling confused about what my observations of seeing Dustin in action meant. And why couldn't I get his hard dick pressed up against me off my mind? Something was going on inside me when it came to him. Was it admiration? Respect? Attraction? Either I couldn't explain it or didn't want to yet.

"You tired?" Dustin interrupted my train of thought as we reached the front porch of our cottage. "Because I most definitely am."

"How can you be tired?" I said. "Unless you're talking about your snoring, which could have kept most of Napa Valley awake."

"You wrong for that, Doc."

"Besides, you weren't the one climbing walls, walking across ropes from treetop to treetop, or trust-falling backward into the arms of the mess known as Wes Jenkins."

We laughed and looked at each other. I was self-conscious, my white Cal U Lake Merced T-shirt dusty, sweat beading at my hairline, me smelling musky, a lot like outside. Dustin, on the other hand, shirtless with his lean arms, shoulders, and abs exposed and slender legs extending from his nylon workout shorts, was definitely of the fit-over-forty club and looked like he could run a marathon even after a full morning facilitating the activities and group discussions.

"I'm sorry you got randomly paired with Wes," Dustin said. He rolled and twirled his wet-with-sweat tank top and snapped it at my side "Sorry, but not sorry. That was funny."

"What are you? Eight years old?" I rolled, twirled, and snapped my towel at Dustin's side. "You need to put your shirt back on. And you're not sorry."

I thought of being a kid and the pranks Markell and I would play on each other after gym or sports practice— snapping towels, wrestling, play fighting, and such. It was often a sign of playful affection among youngsters, to stake out territory, to signal who was stronger. I didn't know adults played these kinds of games with each other, but it definitely felt like flirting on Dustin's part. I had to admit to myself, I didn't mind it.

"You wanna make me put my shirt on?"

"Maybe I want you to keep it off like you did last night." I couldn't believe what I'd said to him. It flowed naturally off my tongue. Thoughts into words would have had me telling him to take the shorts off, too. But I didn't. This was not like me at all. I wasn't a forward person with men. "Anyway, you're good at this retreat stuff. I liked seeing you in your element."

As we made it to the front door, both of us reached out for the handle at the same time, his hand on top of mine. It felt electric.

"After you," we both said simultaneously, not letting go of the door handle for a few seconds, staring at each other until Dustin released his hand from mine.

"You win, Doc," Dustin said as he followed me inside. "He who opens the door first showers first."

"I'll be quick," I said, removing my soiled T-shirt, and throwing it on my open suitcase.

"And don't be taking one of those heaux baths or one of those don't-wash-your-legs showers, Doc," Dustin said and paused. "You hear that?"

"What?"

"I've slipped and called you Doc a few times and you didn't get annoyed, yell at me, tell me to stop. That's progress."

"It's called adulting," I said and let out a chuckle. "It's called we built trust during the weekend retreat."

"It's called being forced to sleep in the same bed unexpectedly."

"It's called I'm a good roommate and bedmate and got you hard," I said. "We shouldn't be doing this. Why are we so silly today?"

Both shirtless, we laughed and leaned against the kitchen counter next to each other. I saw a brief up-and-down glance from him, hoping he'd notice I was a fit-over-forty club member, too, albeit not at the same level as Dustin.

"So, you wanna tell me what do—or did—you like about seeing me in my element with the retreat?"

I shook my head. "Nah, not really." I looked him in the eye and smirked.

"Such an academic tease, Doc."

"You just want me to gas you up, huh, Dustin?"

"Do whatever you want, within reason. I just want you to pick up what I'm trying to put down."

"Here goes, then," I said. "You're very good at what you do. When you're in action, you really take command. You're the total professional package with the analytical part with the report and the on-the-ground practitioner part with retreats. I like that in a person."

"Thank you, Doc," Dustin said, a hint of blush and flattery in his face. "I didn't expect that from you. A compliment. Given our shaky start."

I held a fist up to bump his.

"Willing to forgive. Won't forget. Your future actions will show what you're really about."

"Future?"

"The weeks you have left in the Bay Area working with me, right?"

"That."

"You need to call or visit your mama, too, and let her know you're in town," I said. "How you treat your mama shows how you'll treat other significant people in your life. Even if she has her alleged flaws."

"Look at you being a good influence on me, Doc. When we get back to SF—"

"I mean at our age, in our forties, we're lucky to still have parents who are alive," I said. "Not preaching, though. You're an adult and can make your own decisions. Anyway, we need to shower and get on the road."

Dustin stared at me and said, "I'm enjoying this bonding time with you. Thanks for being open and a good sport. Again, I apologize for Big Dustin getting carried away and turned on this morning."

He leaned over slowly and patted me on the shoulder. Not that I expected more, given the professional relationship and the accreditation work ahead. But we'd shared some moments of intimacy—talking, sharing, disclosing—and all I got was a pat on the shoulder for being a good sport.

Maybe I was reading too much into our breakthrough.

"One more thing," Dustin said as he pulled some toiletries from his duffel bag by the sleeper sofa. "I see you in your element with the Cal U Lake Merced team. They really like and respect you."

"Thanks for the compliment."

"You're going to make a good campus president one day. I can't wait to be there when it happens. Now take your shower so we can get outta here."

A few minutes later, I stood naked in the bathroom with the shower running in the background, hoping the sound muffled me and my video call.

"Markell, what you up to?" I said, cupping my mouth and phone and speaking in a whisper. I was surprised he picked up. He rarely did. "You got a sec?"

"Why are you whispering?" Markell asked. "And why are you FaceTiming me from the bathroom?"

"I have to make it quick," I said. "You busy?"

"Just finished my morning workout," Markell said. The sign for the bus line he took from downtown to Castro was prominent in his background. "About to meet Nate for a movie and lunch before my evening shift at Beaux. Working the US Party tonight. What's up?"

"I have so much to tell you about this weekend," I said. "But let's just say I'm smitten."

"Smitten? What the hell kinda 1950s movies you been watching, Taylor?"

I rolled my eyes at the screen, at Markell.

"Smitten is a vocabulary word for being overwhelmed, maybe struck by someone romantically."

"I graduated from college, too, Taylor," Markell said. "You said you had to make it quick. What's up? I feel weird with you naked on the phone."

"You've seen me naked, bruh."

"My bus about to pull up. What's going on?"

I lowered my voice even more, trying to avoid Dustin from overhearing my conversation with Markell.

"I'll tell you more when I get back to SF from Napa, but in a nutshell, Dustin, D.J., Junior, whatever you call him, and I ended up being paired as roommates this weekend for the work retreat."

"Wait. You gave him some?"

"No, Markell. I did not give him some. But we did sleep in the same bed, and he was bricked up when we woke. It was hot, waking up with him pressed up against me. It was kinda big, too. No, it *was* big. But we didn't do anything like that."

"So, why you being so secretive, calling me from the bathroom?"

"I'll tell you more later," I said. "But Dustin is interesting. He's not too bad. Well, not as bad as we thought initially."

"Wait a second," Markell said. I saw the look of shock and surprise on his face. "Are you telling me that you, Dr. Wannabe College President, is interested in someone?"

"I think that's what I'm saying." I paused and smiled at my bestie. "No, Markell. That's exactly what I'm saying."

CHAPTER EIGHT

Dustin

"You ready to call it a day, bruh?"

I leaned against the doorway of Taylor's office and smiled. I'd packed up my work bag—the one I bought after the smash-and-grab—and was ready to call a car to pick me up from campus to take me back to my hotel in the Castro.

Taylor, looking intelligent and handsome in black reading frames while staring at the screen, looked up from his computer, smiled, and signaled for me to close the door, which I did. Though we had nothing to hide at this point, I knew Taylor did not want to give Wes Jenkins, President Weatherspoon, or other campus colleagues any ammunition to use against him at work.

For several days after the weekend retreat, all I could do was think about Taylor. How much I wanted to be near him, smell him, talk to him, hold him, touch him, kiss him. How much I fantasized about his athleticism and team spirit attitude during the ropes course activities I led. Though we'd done nothing remotely romantic or physical with each other, I knew what I was feeling for Taylor was more than just lust. It was the beautiful essence of him. It was everything about him I knew and everything about him I wanted to know.

We were nearing the halfway point of our work together,

and today, like most days, had been rewarding. My team had spent the afternoon interviewing transgender, nonbinary, and genderqueer students of color, including my cousin Manessa and their performer colleague Coco Hydrate, who were part of a university program Taylor had created to recruit, admit, retain, and graduate that demographic with four-year degrees. I learned a lot about their college experiences, much of which was corroborated in the accreditation report Taylor's team had compiled and submitted. I was eager to learn more about the upcoming marketing campaign to highlight the campus and the program Taylor led to recruit students from states where anti-trans and anti-LGBTQ laws were being passed. I loved their idea of marketing the Cal U Lake Merced campus as a safe haven for people wanting to escape states not supporting their identities.

But that would be a conversation for later.

I had other plans now, which included getting Taylor out of the office at a decent hour.

"You had me in accreditation meetings all day, Dustin," he said, pointing to a tablet, a spiral notebook, and a pile of papers on his desk. "I can't get any work done in meetings, and every meeting produces a to-do list. So, here I am doing to-do list work."

"And here I am to rescue you and give you a break." I sat my bag on a chair and walked behind Taylor at his desk. I put my hands on his shoulders, a little more than just a pat, but less than a squeeze or massage. Couldn't tell if it was tension or muscle I was feeling, but all I knew was I was close to Taylor, and he wasn't pushing me away. "Is this all right with you?"

"It's not right," he said. "It's not wrong."

Taylor leaned his face down toward the desk. I rubbed his knotted-up shoulders a little more before stopping. Didn't want to risk anyone coming into Taylor's office and seeing us like this.

"You ready?"

Taylor lifted his head up from the desk.

"Ready for what?"

"I want to take you somewhere special, if that's all right."

"You wanna tell me where we're going?"

"Then that's a yes? You're gonna be surprised and pleased and well fed, I promise."

Forty minutes later, after sitting in rush-hour traffic on the Bay Bridge and some combination of the 80, 580, and 880 freeways through Oakland, our rideshare pulled up in front of the modest house I grew up in. The neighborhood, while still rough around the edges and somewhat hood, was beginning to show signs of rebirth and reinvestment. I'd noticed a few new condo buildings, coffee shops, exercise studios, and restaurants as we were riding through. They were mixed in with the older, non-refurbished buildings. Bike lanes and parks sat where abandoned stolen cars and drug deals used to be the norm when I was growing up.

"I called my mama after the retreat weekend," I said as I pushed a few buttons on my phone to complete the transaction to pay the rideshare driver. "She asked me to come to dinner. So, I brought you."

"Whaaaaa?" Taylor said. "I'm glad you're talking to her. But this is a lot. Our first hangout and meeting your mom."

I squeezed Taylor's shoulder. "I need you here for moral support. Plus, she won't act a complete fool in front of company."

We retrieved our work bags from the trunk, and my mama yelled excitedly from her front porch, as if I couldn't hear her, "Hey, baby. Hey, Junior."

"Here goes nothing," I whispered to Taylor. "She's so freaking loud."

"Be nice, Junior," he whispered back to me and winked an eye. "You only get one mom."

"Hey, Mama," I yelled back. "Good to see you."

"See, you're doing good," Taylor whispered to me. I appreciated the reassurance from him. "What do I call her?"

"Ms. McMillan is fine. Though she'll say to call her Kim—or Lil' Kim. She gets a kick out of that."

"All right then," Taylor said. "You got this. I'm here. I can be your excuse to leave early."

"Thanks, I appreciate that," I said as we reached the porch, where I hugged my mom. I noticed she still went to the old-school hairdressers who worked out of a kitchen, her head full of neat rows of small, tight roller curls. I loved seeing how the outdoor furniture I'd ordered for the front area complemented the new exterior I'd had constructed. "Ma, Taylor. Taylor, Ms. McMillan."

My mama grabbed Taylor and yelled out, loud enough for the whole neighborhood to hear, "Taylor, I don't shake hands, I hug." She pulled Taylor into her arms and laughed. "You can call me Kim—or Lil' Kim. I'm a junior, too, just like Junior here, except I had a relationship with my mama, and Junior's daddy is a piece of shit that barely showed his face around here, though he had another family just up the street. That's why I gave Junior my last name, but made sure his wife knew who Dustin was from with his first name."

I rolled my eyes and gave Taylor the look that said "here we go" as we entered her house.

"Ma, are you using any of the Nordstrom gift cards I send to you?"

"Junior, I don't go nowhere but the casino and the grocery store. What's wrong with what I got on?"

"Nothing," Taylor said and smiled. "You look beautiful, Mrs. Mc…I mean Kim."

I mouthed "thank you" to Taylor as we made our way farther inside.

My investment in home improvements for her paid off. Though this was the house I'd grown up in, it did not resemble anything I remembered. It was an HGTV makeover dream house—the floors, the fixtures, the furniture—and I was glad my mom had a clean, modern place to live as she got older. Safe, too, apparently, as there were no more burglar bars on the exterior windows and she and everyone else had Ring cameras and direct lines to law enforcement. I guess the neighborhood was changing. Slowly. Made withdrawing from my 401(k) plan with my previous consulting job feel worth it, even though the taxes killed me.

Mama made what seemed like three Sunday dinners on a random Thursday night for Taylor and me, with platters of fried catfish, fried and baked chicken, and fried pork chops on one side of the island counter and pans of greens, black-eyed peas, spaghetti, cheese grits, and macaroni and cheese on the other side, along with pitchers of the party punch she used to make—one with red Kool-Aid, one with sweet tea. One thing for sure, my mom still knew how to make her way around a kitchen, even when we were growing up with next to nothing and her love.

"Ma, who you cook all this for? It's just you staying here, right?"

"Junior, I keeps a man," she said. "But I wanted to make sure y'all got some good home cooking. Looking like skin and bones. I know you ain't had a real meal staying in that hotel. You know you can stay with me."

Which was true. But I didn't want to. And I didn't want to go there with the conversation.

For the most part, Taylor stayed silent unless asked something directly. I guessed it was out of being mannerable and polite, and that was fine with me. Kept his conversation mostly to compliments about the dinner she'd made for us, even when my mom asked embarrassing questions or brought up unmentionable topics.

"I don't get how the gays these days be in they forties and ain't got a belly, titties, or extra chins at that age," she said, laughing. "Back in my day, forties meant married and fat, with three kids, and sniffing around me when the wife ain't wanna give it up no more to his fat ass."

"Ma. Too much information."

"Hey, Taylor," my mom shouted next to us. "I heard you just moved here to the Bay Area recently. I don't know how y'all stand living there anymore without any Blacks in the city. Well, the mayor, bless her. How you afford to stay in the city? What you do again?"

"Ma!"

"Chile, there once was a time when I lived in them streets in San Francisco—the Fillmore District, Bayview-Hunters Point. The clubs, restaurants, and stores, all Black-owned. The bookstores and poetry scene—you know Maya Angelou lived here before she was *the* Maya Angelou. They called Fillmore the Harlem of the West. Our hip-hop scene. Vallejo. Oakland, too. Google it. At one time, we was almost fifteen, twenty percent of San Francisco. The whole Bay Area lost its soul and quirky attitude when they let tech take over, and now tech trying to sneak out after reaping the benefits. But let me shut up. What do I know?"

"You know a lot because you lived it," Taylor said. "I'll research it, Ms. McMillan."

"Junior. How your little dancer friend Silas doing?"

I wondered how much red party punch Ma had gotten into before Taylor and I arrived. Her censorship button was not on, as I'd predicted.

"Ma, we don't talk about him. We not together like that anymore."

"You know he comes to check on me since you moved away after the pandemic," she said. "Bought me this new 'frigerator."

"Good, but you don't have to talk to Silas anymore. And the fridge that came with the remodeling should have still been under warranty."

"It's a long story, baby," she said, and then she shook her head like she'd had a revelation. "Wait, is Taylor your new little friend?"

"Ma."

"Is this the one who got Man-Man and Cornelius into the college? You the Docta Taylor they be talking about when they come around here?"

"Ma. Man-Man goes by Manessa now. Cornelius is Coco Hydrate now."

"Y'all and all these pronouns and gender stuff. I'm open minded, but it's too much alphabet soup to keep up with. But I'm glad times are changing for y'all. Back in my day, they sent you away or forced you to marry someone for appearances' sake."

"Ma. It's easy if you listen and want to learn."

Ma grabbed my hand. "How come you ain't call me when you got to town? I heard it's been three or four weeks since you been back in the Bay Area."

"Ma. This project I'm working on with Taylor been keeping me busy. I'll see you before I head back to Chicago."

"When is that?"

"A few more weeks," I said. "I'll be back. We'll be back."

"Got your little track and field scholarship to college and just kept on running all over the U.S. and away from here."

"You wouldn't understand. You didn't try to."

"Anyway…"

She pulled away and walked over to the kitchen pantry, where she pulled out Styrofoam containers, aluminum foil, and plastic utensils and cups. Changed the subject like always.

"Before y'all go back to San Francisco, make you a to-go plate or two. Y'all say it's healthy and being fit, but y'all look a little too skinny to me. Y'all not doing coke, right?"

"No, Ma, we're definitely not doing coke," I said, embarrassed she'd even ask us something like that. "I'm still running and working out."

"Definitely no coke, Ms. McMillan," Taylor said. "Just long days of meetings, not a lot of eating, but I make a mean smoothie to keep me going throughout the day."

"Y'all gone waste away with all this professional busyness and trying to keep up your youth. But who am I? Just a mama."

I watched my ma plate up our food, get hers in plastic storage containers, and load the dishwasher in the span of a few minutes, it seemed.

"Thanks, Ma, for the food, though. It's getting late. We got work in the morning."

"Before you go, baby, can I hold fifty dollars till I get my check on the first?"

"I'll app you a couple hundred, Ma. Keep it."

"Can you put something on Dorian's books at Solano, while you at it?"

"I do every week, Ma, like clockwork."

"Thanks, baby," she said. "He appreciates it and so do I. Y'all look cute together, whatever you are. Hope you happy. Come by again before you leave town."

"All right, Ma."

"You know I'm proud of you. No matter how far you run or stay away from here."

Twenty-five minutes later, with little traffic heading west, we'd crossed the Bay Bridge back into San Francisco. Taylor and I sat in silence, looked at the bright lights of downtown on both side of the bridge, and listened to slow jams on KBLX radio that our rideshare driver had on. We'd agreed to share costs on the ride and put in our respective stops—his at his place near the Lake Merced campus, and then mine at the Hotel Castro. When we arrived at Taylor's building, I asked the driver if we could get charged for fifteen minutes' wait time while I helped Taylor inside the lobby with his work bag, the to-go plates, and jacket.

"Don't worry about making the driver wait," Taylor said. "We'll call you another car when you leave. I want to talk about dinner."

I was a nervous wreck in the elevator heading up to Taylor's place. Nervous about his impressions of my mama. Nervous about how he thought I'd reacted to her. Nervous about being invited into his space. He had to have had a clue about how I felt by now. Not everyone curates a first hangout with their date and their mom.

Taylor's apartment was compact, but the panoramic corner windows looking out into the dark sky, ocean, and lake made it appear larger than it was. It was tidy but not obnoxiously clean, and smelled good, much like the signature soap and cocoa butter scent that was Taylor. I reminded myself to ask him his scent secret.

"Excuse the appearance," Taylor said. He sat his things on a bench near the front desk and motioned for me to set mine near his. "Housekeeper comes on Sundays. I'm not the best at keeping it up during the week. Busy with work, you know."

"It's fine," I said. "I'm the same. My poor plants. I hope they survive me being away so long from Chicago. My neighbor has a key, though…"

"Poor plants."

"You stay alone here, Doc?" I asked. "We're alone?"

"Yeah, I'm one of the lucky ones that doesn't have to have a roommate or housemate to make ends meet."

"Consider yourself lucky. It's why I think most people get into situationships or delusionships in the Bay Area. Too damn expensive." I paused. "Your place is cute. It's you."

"I'll take that as a compliment, I guess."

We stood in silence a few seconds. My heart was beating a million miles a minute. I couldn't believe Taylor'd invited me inside his apartment. I didn't want to fumble the bag.

"Apologies for my mom."

"She's absolutely delightful, and I had fun." He seemed sincere, so I believed him. "Thanks for inviting me. I needed a break from work and from San Francisco. I hate I don't get to Oakland as much as I could and should. Guess I got that 'if I have to cross a bridge, I'm not going' mentality."

"That can be changed," I said. "Now that you see what, where, and who I come from, what do you think? As you can see, I ain't come from much. Ain't got no three generations of college pedigree like you. Probably why I want only the best now that I got the means. Anyway, I'm rambling. Sorry."

"Don't worry about it, Dustin," Taylor said. "Parents can be a lot sometimes. We'll probably be a lot when we have our own kids. Not we, as in us, you and me. We, in general."

"Gotcha. We, in general."

"I didn't know you had a brother who was locked up."

"Yeah, long story. Does that bother you?"

Taylor reached out and grabbed one of my hands.

"Not at all," Taylor said. "I mean, I've got questions and

there's plenty of time for answers. But you're amazing, Dustin. Nothing to be embarrassed about."

"You're amazing, too, Taylor." We smiled at each other and stared. Both our hands were entwined, and neither of us was letting go. There was no doubt what was happening in my mind, but I needed to know what Taylor thought. "Can I ask or tell you something?"

"Of course."

"I'm trying not to read things the wrong way…"

"You're not."

"And I know I started off on the wrong foot."

"You did."

Why did Taylor have to make this difficult for me, make me work for what I had been leading up to? I deserved it, I guessed. But he hadn't moved, and our hands were still together. So, I gave my shot.

"I like you."

Silence. Silence. Silence.

I could feel my heart beating, breath getting shallow, sweat forming at my forehead and hairline. Started regretting opening up, being vulnerable, sharing a feeling with Taylor. Wondered if I'd misread things over these weeks working together—the glances, the smiles, the compliments, the flattery, the conversations. Regardless, one thing I knew. It wasn't like me, Dustin McMillan, to get rejected. I usually saw, pursued, and attained. But there I stood, getting nothing back from Taylor. No reaction. Nothing. I mean lowkey, he wasn't even my type, compared to the dancers, track, and basketball type guys I'd been with over the years. I could and should have bolted from Taylor's place right then, but I had too much stuff to carry, a car to call, and time to wait to be picked up.

"You cool people," Taylor said. "I like you, too."

Relieved. Relieved. Relieved. I inhaled and exhaled.

"Damn, bruh," I said. "Keep a man waiting, guessing."

We laughed. Stared. Moved closer to each other, while standing in the foyer of Taylor's apartment. I imagined how Taylor's full lips and mustache would feel against mine. I could smell remnants of the breath mints we'd both chewed on while riding back to San Francisco, attempting to cover up the seasonings, aromas, and flavors of tonight's dinner. As I closed in on Taylor, my phone rang—my mom's ringtone.

"My mama, ugh. Talk about killing the mood. Hold on."

"All good. Tell her hello and good night for me. And thanks for all the food. I really appreciate it and her hospitality. I'll be eating good for days."

Taylor stepped back and started putting his things away around the apartment while I took the call from my mom.

"Yeah, Ma, I made it back...He had a good time, he said...Yes, we'll come back, maybe for a Sunday service and dinner...I have a few more weeks left here...Okay, you're welcome. Let me know if you need more, Ma...I won't forget Dorian's money...Good night...Okay, good night...Bye."

Taylor emerged from what I assumed was his bedroom and got within my orbit again. I heard music by Solange playing from wherever he'd been during my phone call.

"Hey, come here," I called out, putting my arms around Taylor when he was within range. "Where were we, Doc?"

"I think *you* were about to kiss me."

"Oh, is that so?"

"Mm-hmm."

We stared at each other, smiled, and took in each other's faces. Eyes. Noses. Mustaches and beards. Hairlines and haircuts. I interrupted the moment and playfully flicked my index finger on his nose.

"I have wanted to kiss you for so long, Taylor."

"I've grown to want to kiss you. Didn't want anything to do with you in the beginning, to be honest."

"I feel like every time I made a step forward, you took a step back."

"And now we've both taken a step forward."

"True." I pulled Taylor in closer to me. My pants were getting tight up front, much like that morning in the retreat cabin, excited and in anticipation of what the evening brought so far and could bring later.

"What are you waiting for?" Taylor lowered his eyelids in a sultry way, voice deepened and softened. "We're alone. In my place. No roommates. We're adults. We like each other. You still like me, right, Dustin?"

"Of course."

I traced my index finger softly along his top and lower lips. Gently moved my lips toward Taylor's cheek. He slowly moved his face toward me so that our lips grazed, first hesitantly, then, with comfort and confidence growing, fervently. Relaxed, we pulled closer in our embrace. His hands graced the back of my neck, mine on his face, and our mouths opened and figured out the rhythm of kissing someone new for the first time.

I thought this couldn't have been real. It had to have been a dream. But it wasn't. We pulled away from each other's lips slightly but kept our noses touching, our warm breath an indicator of the heat that rose between us.

"How are you feeling, Doc?" I muttered against his lips. "You good?"

"Better than good."

"Oh yeah?"

"Yeah."

Taylor pulled me into him and backed us against the foyer wall. More kisses turned into grinding. I bent slightly and turned my attention to his neck, planting baby kisses and tiny licks up and down while he panted and whimpered and beckoned softly for me not to stop. By then, I knew he had to have felt the excitement I had for him, as my stiffness protruded and pressed against his, which I definitely felt. Taylor ran his hands lower down my back until he slid them inside the back pockets of my slacks, pulling me even closer.

We moaned, groped, kissed, panted, touched, and breathed while against the wall for several minutes, until I wondered if Taylor was ready for more. I pulled my face from Taylor's and smiled. He smiled back and leaned in again.

"What are we doing?" Taylor whispered against my lips.

"Being adults."

"You're so hot, Dustin."

"So are you, Doc. I've wanted you from the moment I first saw you."

I pulled Taylor's hands from my back pockets and held them next to him against the wall.

He kissed me again. "You wanna go for it tonight? I've got plenty of lube and condoms. I'm on PrEP, too."

"So am I—and I do wanna go for it." I pulled away from Taylor, putting just a little space between us. "Damn, I do."

"I can tell," Taylor said as he looked down at my dick print swinging a hard left in my pants. "Yum."

"You, yum, too." I ran my hand along his dick print, which offered much to anticipate.

"You did that," Taylor said, eyelids lowered again. "Sexy Dustin."

"But maybe we can or should do this another time," I said, pulling away some more. Not that I wanted to stop. Knowing how much I wanted Taylor, physically and mentally, I didn't want to stop wanting him after some spontaneous sex and an orgasm. Though I'd had my fair share of one-and-done experiences with men over the years, Taylor was different to me. Adult. Mature. Age appropriate. On the same level. Experienced. Intelligent. The kind I'd see myself with beyond one night, even though that was my initial goal with Taylor when we met at Beaux. I started adjusting myself in my pants. I couldn't believe what I was saying, what I was doing…or not doing. Between the two of us, I was sure it would have been Taylor being the rational one and calling it a night. "Like when it's not so late at night."

"Yeah," Taylor said. "Or when we haven't eaten so much. I don't want us painting the sheets…my sheets."

We both laughed.

"Or when we haven't worked all day and haven't had a chance to shower," I said. "Though I like my men smelling fresh like soap and cocoa butter, or smelling a little ripe sometimes."

"Oh yeah?" Taylor raised an eyebrow at me.

"Yeah."

"Dirty boy," Taylor said. "I can't wait to learn what else you like, Dustin."

"I can't wait to teach and learn from you, Doc. Experience higher education at its best."

"Oh yeah, definitely hands-on learning," Taylor said. He pulled me in one more time for a kiss. We left it at a peck and a hug. "Wait till I show you how slutty and dirty and passionate this academic good boy can be."

I pulled away reluctantly, again. This time for good for the night. I exhaled a deep breath, not in relief, but in disbelief we'd stopped what we'd started.

"Okay, I better go," I said and pressed the app for a rideshare. A car was four minutes away, which gave me enough time to gather my things and head to the elevator and down to the lobby.

"Thanks for a good night, Dustin," Taylor said. "It meant a lot."

"Thank you, I had fun." I gave Taylor a quick kiss on the mouth before I told him good night, picked up my bags and jacket, and left his apartment. I had to get out quickly or else who knew what we'd have gotten into that night. When the door closed behind me, I turned around and pressed my hand against it. I was very much still hard, still aroused, and wondered if I'd regret not spending the night with Taylor.

But the car was downstairs. We had work in the morning at the university. And now that we'd shared our feelings, and given in a little to our desires, I knew an even tougher job was ahead—one Taylor and I would need to discuss very soon.

How we were going to keep how we felt under wraps while in our meetings and interviews and also while under the watchful eyes of Taylor's work nemesis, Wes Jenkins?

Because there was no way I was gonna stop these feelings for Taylor. Not. now.

CHAPTER NINE

Taylor

"Hey you," I said to Dustin as he stepped into my office doorway at the end of the workday the next day. I motioned for him to come in and shut the office door in case Wes Jenkins was lurking nearby. "I couldn't stop thinking about last night."

"I couldn't either," Dustin said. "Being with Wes Jenkins all day today, though, put a damper on that. He's too much. I don't know how you do it."

Dustin and I hadn't seen each other for much of the day. I'd gotten pulled into helping the president's office resolve a crisis situation with a student organization threatening to protest and take over Merced Hall. I had to leave accreditation work to Wes Jenkins and the team. It was just after five o'clock, and I was close to getting ready to leave.

"What did he do today?" I asked. In our profession, it wasn't the actual work that was problematic. It was people and personalities like Wes Jenkins that made university work hard. "I'm sorry for you having to be around him all day."

"Let's not talk about it. I'll be all right. It's *you* I worry about."

"If you say so," I said. "What do you mean?"

"You need to keep your guard up and eyes open around

Wes Jenkins. He's trouble. I should have known better when I started getting a bunch of revised versions of your accreditation report days before getting into town. But that's water under the bridge. I care about you and your career, and someone like Wes Jenkins does not."

"You know how hard it is to get rid of bad people in a university, though."

"Believe me, I know. Same in corporate and tech life, too," Dustin said. "But don't be so up in the clouds doing good for everyone and seeing the good in everyone that you don't see when they are not good for you. All right?"

"I hear you," I said. "Sounds like you've had your fair share of office politics, huh?"

"Office, family, love, life politics, all of it," Dustin said. "But this ain't about me now, Doc. You're a good guy. I care about what happens to you."

I smiled and shrugged my shoulders. I knew he was speaking truth. I knew something had to be done about Wes Jenkins. Maybe once accreditation was over, I'd broach the topic with President Weatherspoon. But until then, I'd deal.

"Thanks, Dustin," I said. "I appreciate that."

He came close to my work table, grabbed my left hand, kissed the top of it, and said, "I care. And I'm keeping it innocent and professional at work, like you requested."

"Thanks."

"But back to our initial conversation topic, Doc. I was thinking about you all day, too."

"You're sweet."

"You're sweeter." Dustin sat in the guest chair near the door, legs open and stretched out, arms crossed behind his head, eyes closed. "I'm happy the workday is over and it's the weekend."

I eyed him up and down and bit my bottom lip as my

gaze casually zeroed in on the bulge between his legs of his tight suit pants. If we weren't in the office, I'd have kneeled in front of him and sucked the end-of-the-workweek tension out of him then and there. But the time would come, eventually, to take care of Dustin.

I didn't want to assume anything, like we'd be spending any or all of the weekend together, so I asked, "Any plans?"

Dustin jerked back to attention and immediately ran through all the things he wanted to do over the weekend. What he shared included trying out a new rooftop lounge opening in the Mission District, catching a newly released film at the big new movie theater downtown, and hiking near the ocean in Pacifica. Then he joked, "I was going to ask this guy out, but I'm a little nervous. I don't want to get rejected."

"Oh yeah?" I asked, a hint of sarcasm in my voice. "Who is this guy?"

"Some Black, brilliant boss who's on the team that's running some university in San Francisco. Maybe you've heard of this guy, Dr. Taylor James? Grew up in this storybook, perfect, Black excellence family with some coins in L.A."

We smiled at each other, our eyes lingering in the quiet of the office and the peace of being alone together. I wanted to kiss and a whole lot more with him, pick up where we'd left off the night before. For now, staring at each other would have to suffice while on campus, even in my closed-door office.

"You sound booked and busy, Dr. Dustin McMillan," I said. "I wonder if there'll be enough time to fit in this Dr. James guy this weekend?"

Dustin smiled.

"Oh, I'ma fit it in all right."

"Is that so? I don't know."

"You know what, Doc? I made all that stuff up," he said. "I ain't got no agenda. Just be back at my hotel. But I do want to spend time with you this weekend. Not monopolize your time. But spend time."

"I'd like that."

"So, grown man shit," he said. "We've had moments and hangouts and a hot make-out session, but not a real date date. You and me. So, how do you want to be asked out? What makes Dr. Taylor James happy on a date? What makes a good date for you?"

"Deep questions, huh?"

"Tell me."

It had been years since I'd had what looked like a burgeoning relationship, let alone a first date or a good date. I explained the meaningless entanglements of my young and slutty twenties, the string of conference hookups with academic rock stars whose work I'd admired, read, and quoted in my thirties, and the decision to chill on all aspects of physical and romantic relationships in my forties because of my career focus.

"I've had very few first real dates, and never a boyfriend or partner. Even at my age, believe it or not. I mean, nothing is wrong with me. People like to imply something's wrong. Time just flew by. Here I am. I don't have game. I don't have swag. I'm handsome, but not hot. All I have is intelligence and professionalism and a good heart. And I'm rambling and embarrassed for saying all this."

"All good," Dustin said. "You are perfect to me, in this time and space. To be honest, intelligence, a good sense of self, riveting conversations, and stability are more meaningful to me than fun, sex, sexuality, and getting run though. Doesn't matter to me you ain't had a man."

"Thank you. I appreciate that. I've never really voiced this about me. I'm not embarrassed, but I am embarrassed. If that makes sense."

"I will hold it and not violate it. You safe with me, Doc."

"Thanks."

"But you ain't answer my question," he said. "How can I be a good first date to you?"

I appreciated Dustin's patience and persistence with me. It was something I didn't have a ready answer for and hadn't thought of. Because I never had to. Or just didn't.

"Here goes," I said. "I make decisions all day at work. I make decisions all evening when I get home. I gotta decide dinner, my errands, when to take the trash and recycling out. I am decision fatigued. I want someone to say, 'Be ready at this time,' or 'I'm bringing a bottle of wine and having Minnie Bell's sent to your place,' or 'The Beyoncé concert is next weekend and I have two tickets and I want to take you to Paris to see her,' or 'Let me take care of everything, so you don't have to do anything,' you know what I mean, Dustin? And not in a controlling way. Because I'm too independent to be controlled."

"I know exactly what you mean." He got up and walked over to my workstation, holding up my left hand and kissing it. "That's very helpful."

"Is it?" I said. I felt relieved and excited to open up about this part of my life with Dustin. "I've never shared. No one's ever asked."

"That's deep questions and deep answers, too," he said, keeping my hand in his. "So how about this? I'll pack an overnight bag, if that's okay since I'm tired of hotel living, and I'll be at your place at seven. I can get us reservations at this Black-owned barber and spa joint in the Fillmore District, because we both need fresh haircuts and edge ups, and a massage would do us both good. Then we can figure out dinner and stream something at your place tonight. Maybe Ava DuVernay's *Origin*. We can play the rest of the weekend by ear, and if you want some space, just let me know and I'll go. If you want to hang out some more, we can. Again, I don't want to monopolize your weekend, but I know my time in San Francisco is winding down in a couple weeks, and—"

A ringtone pierced the conversation. We both looked at our phones and devices. Nothing. It sounded again. We realized it was outside my office door. I shushed Dustin, he did the same to me, and we stayed still for a few seconds or so. A few seconds later, we heard the sound of footsteps walking away from my office toward the elevator.

I got up and opened the door.

"You got a problem, Wes Jenkins?" I'd gotten up so quickly that he'd barely made it ten feet from my office door.

"Uh, no. I thought I heard voices and didn't know anyone else was here." Wes stayed put and didn't move away or toward my office.

"Were you listening?"

"Oh geez no. I've got more going on in my life than wondering what's going on in yours," Wes said. "I'm staying on campus late tonight. Justin Monroe's BlaQueer Club is hosting an event, and they asked me to attend. Nothing major."

"Next time you want to know if I'm in the office late, just text me or send me a Teams message, Wes Jenkins. You got that?"

Wes continued down the hall, and I slammed my office door once inside.

"I like not-nice Taylor," Dustin said. "I'm telling you, it's hot when you're more of yourself. Not that being nice isn't yourself. You know what I'm saying."

"Maybe it's time to get out of here." I looked at my phone for the time. "Text me when you're on the way or outside my building. I'll be ready."

❖

Hours later, with freshly cut and faded hair, relaxed muscles, and a plastic bag with containers of leftover sushi, Dustin and I arrived back at my apartment just before midnight. We took off our shoes inside the front door, put our jackets on the bench in the foyer, and Dustin explored the living room.

"Come over here," he said to me after I put our leftovers in the refrigerator. He was standing at the expansive windows, looking out at the darkness of the Pacific, pierced with a few lights of ships floating slowly in the distance. I stood behind him and put my arms around his waist from behind. He held my hands against his gray hoodie, which matched his gray sweats. Must be his go-to casual outfit. He also wore it for our morning at Chrissy Field and Golden Gate Bridge weeks ago. "I bet this view looks great in the light."

"It's beautiful at sunset," I said. "When I'm able to catch it and am at home. I get some beautiful golden hour selfies. Not that I'm shallow like that or anything."

"It's a sign of the times…selfies," he said. "I can't wait to see the sunset from here."

"You will."

"Oh yeah?"

I kissed the back left side of Dustin's neck. "You're beautiful right now." I planted more kisses on his neck and ears. "Is this okay?"

"More than okay."

"You're okay staying here tonight?"

"Absolutely," Dustin said. "You okay with me staying?"

"We have to finish what we started last time you were here," I said. "There's more where that came from."

Dustin unhooked my hands from around his waist, turned around, and traced my freshly lined and newly-grown-in beard with his hands. He pulled me toward him and kissed me. Breathlessly. Confidently. Eagerly.

There, in front of the window with the dark Pacific Ocean as our backdrop in the distance, I received his warm kisses over my lips, face, and neck. Kisses that signaled the start of something new. Kisses that signaled a night to anticipate. Kisses that signaled two grown men who were falling into each other.

I could feel our excitement growing in our pants as we pulled and pressed closer, our hands in each other's back pockets. I moaned and he grunted as we savored tongues, mouths, and skin. I reached down, pulled his hoodie over his head, and tossed it on the nearby sofa. He pulled my polo off and let it slide to the hardwood floor. There, bare-chested, we gave ourselves more body canvas to admire, touch, kiss, and lick for the first time. My hot mouth greedily savored his skin, tracing the outline of his many chest and arm tattoos with my tongue. Dustin sucked in with pleasure, as skin to skin, chest to chest, waist to waist, the heat rose between us.

"Couch," I breathed against Dustin's ear. I pulled him with me toward the sofa, just feet away from us. "You're excited, huh?"

I sat down first, his dick on brick at high noon at my face, and I put my mouth on the fabric of his sweats where I could see he was hard, and blew hot air.

"Fuuuccccckkkk, that feels so warm, so good." Dustin moaned and writhed for a few seconds as he gently ran his fingers across the side of my face and beard. "Stop, stop, stop. Let me take care of you first."

"Your choice, Dustin."

He pushed me back on the sofa and planked over me. He

kissed my lips again, then lower to my neck and even farther down to my pecs and nipples while unfastening my pants. He reached in, pulled it out, and inserted me in his mouth all before I realized what was happening. I saw myself disappearing into his mouth. Usually, I could tell within a few licks or seconds if someone was going to be good at head. Dustin was a pro, and I loved it. I was eager to show him how good I could be at it.

A few minutes later he pulled off me, stood up slowly, and helped me get off the sofa. Our hands roaming ferociously, I used my feet to wrestle out of my pants and underwear, which were pooled at my ankles. I tugged his sweats and boxer briefs from around his hard-on and slowly slid them down and off.

"I want you so bad, Doc," he said.

"I want you, too."

"*Show* me."

"Show *me*."

We kissed slowly. Pulled away. Looked at each other, smiled, hugged, and kissed again.

"You ready for this?"

"I'm more than ready," I said as I took one of Dustin's hands, his other around my waist, and led him slowly toward my bedroom, where we'd spend the next couple days together in hot and sweaty bliss. "The movie will have to wait."

CHAPTER TEN

Dustin

I woke up startled, forgetting I was at Taylor's apartment and not at my hotel room in the Castro. Once I realized where I was, I rolled over to look at him and put my arms around him to big spoon him again, but saw only the view of Lake Merced and daylight entering through his bedroom window.

"Doc?" I called out, wondering where he was.

Surely, he hadn't gotten bored of me, being one of those people who hosts who wakes up early and leaves the bed as a hint that they want you out of their place. I hoped that wasn't the case. Not that everything was completely perfect with us these first nights together. It never really is the first few times being with someone, when you're learning each other's bodies, rhythms, likes, and sensitivities together, but we'd definitely had passionate and pleasurable times. And I wanted more, if Taylor did.

I looked around Taylor's bedroom, which was a nice size and decorated simply. Didn't see or hear him in the en suite bathroom. Wasn't in the walk-in closet either. But I did see the remains of our weekend together—linens strewn everywhere, comforter half on the bed, half on the floor. I peeked underneath where we'd slept and saw no paint or remnants, and breathed a sigh of relief. I'd offer to help clean and change the linens if he wanted my help throughout the weekend.

Couldn't remember if it was Saturday or Sunday, since we'd spent most of the weekend in bed, except for a couple of food deliveries here and there and showers, both together and separately. Noticed an old-fashioned digital alarm clock on Taylor's nightstand and realized it was almost eight in the morning. Time for me to take PrEP and my vitamins. Since everything—my phone, boxer briefs, change of clothes, overnight bag with my PrEP pills—was still in the living room after the weekend together, I had no choice but to get up and walk naked to the foyer.

I heard Beyoncé's "Plastic Off the Sofa" playing softly on the living room speakers. Taylor was singing along to it and sounding pretty good carrying the tune when I emerged from the bedroom. He was standing shirtless but with some neon pink sweat shorts, looking handsome as always in the kitchen. He was cooking, and it smelled delicious. When he heard my footsteps, he looked up from the pot where he was stirring something. I loved how his eyes and smile lit up when he saw me. I hoped mine did the same.

"Good morning, Doc," I said. I'm sure I was cheesing like a teenager in like with someone for the first time. "It's our song—well, the one we never got to hear or see performed at drag brunch that day with all my family drama."

"And because cheap tipper moi left the show early," Taylor said. He laughed and put a lid on something on the stove. "Good morning, handsome."

"I came to find some clean boxers and take my PrEP."

"Hey, let me greet you properly." He walked over to naked me in the foyer. I got a whiff of his signature soap and cocoa butter aroma as he put a hand on my shoulder and gave me a peck. I embraced him and gave him a kiss, morning breath and all, and felt myself getting hard again as I pressed against him.

"Someone's excited again, I see," he said.

"I am." I swatted Taylor's ass. "Big Dustin likes Big Taylor."

"Yum." Taylor licked my bottom lip. "Maybe you'll get a quickie after you brush your teeth and take your PrEP. I did both already."

I noticed Taylor had neatly folded my sweats, hoodie, and boxers from the weekend and set them on the bench in the foyer near my overnight bag. Wondered what that meant. An offer of a quickie, my stuff at the front door, and breakfast ready? I hoped this wasn't a one-and-done weekend in Taylor's mind, because it definitely wasn't for me.

I tried not to overthink it as I got myself together in the bathroom. Taylor and I'd had a beautiful and unexpected weekend together at his place. I needed a break from hotel life, restaurant food, and club music bellowing in the Castro District air. He and I, waking together like this, was exactly what I'd wanted from him all those weeks ago when I'd first met him at Beaux, from when we started working together on the university accreditation process. He was exactly the kind of man I wanted to be with. Surprisingly, it seemed to be coming together.

Again, I willed myself not to overthink when I returned to the living room, shirtless and freeballing in black basketball shorts. Taylor hadn't said anything about wanting me to leave or about this being a one-time thing for him, so nothing to be worried about. I plugged in my phone near the bench, noticing I'd missed a few texts and notifications I planned to check in a few. I saw a couple cups of coffee, plates of fruit, and bowls of oatmeal on the island in the kitchen.

"Oatmeal? For real? Did you throw in some extra flaxseed and fiber for show, Doc?" I chuckled. "After everything we did to each other over the weekend?"

"Ahh, shit…literally. I'm just acting out of Sunday routine. I'll save this for myself for tomorrow morning. But at least have some coffee, water, or whatever else you want to get your day started."

I grabbed Taylor's hand and pulled him near me at the island.

"All I want is you. And we ain't gotta do a quickie. When we do it, I want the long version. Like last night, all day yesterday, and the night before that."

"You're such a bad boy, Dustin." He gave me a peck on the lips. "Let's talk about this."

Taylor led me to the sofa, where we'd done fun and naughty things to each other the past few days and nights. My mind raced with excitement and nerves.

"I think I know what you're gonna say, Doc." I put my hands in front of my face like a steeple. "I could tell by you not being in the bedroom when I woke up and from my stuff being stacked by the front door. You want me gone. You not ready for this."

I hadn't usually been the one in this position, being all deferential in these one-and-done, come-and-go, hi-and-bye situationships. I was the confident one, the cocky one, the conceited one who initiated what I wanted, the one who told a trick to leave. People followed my lead. Here, I felt bamboozled, boomeranged with Taylor. Here, I was the one coming across as pleading and needy. A revelation indeed.

Taylor grabbed my hands and took them in his. "What are you really asking or saying, Dustin?"

"I might be in my feelings a little bit," I said. "I'm feeling you. Been feeling you from the moment I first saw you. I've opened up to you in ways I never really do with anyone. I like it and in ways that make me feel vulnerable. That ain't like me, bruh."

"Okay, I see."

"So, if you just want this to be professional, I understand, and as soon as I get a shower, I can be gone."

Taylor squeezed my hands. "I love all of this you're saying, Dustin. I'm in my feelings, too, and I have some for you."

"That's a relief," I said. I'm sure I was blushing, too.

"Yes, I want you gone," Taylor said. "But it's not for the reasons you think. First, I got up early to video chat with my parents in L.A. before they went to church, I checked my work email and tidied up the living room. You were sleeping so peacefully, I didn't want to disturb you. By the way, no Silas dreams or shouts this weekend."

"Oh, I see you ain't forgot," I said, relieved that I hadn't mentioned my ex intentionally or mistakenly over the weekend. "Well, thanks for letting me sleep in a bit."

"The person who cleans my apartment comes on Sundays, and I haven't had overnight company here when they come—not that I'm embarrassed or ashamed or anything, just don't want to surprise them yet with you."

"Gotcha."

"And I kinda have a to-do list today. NAACP meeting at Third Baptist. I signed up to volunteer at an event for the Castro District Arts Council, related to drag and book bans in some local school district, with the city's Drag Laureate coming. And I'm gonna try and make it to Markell's shift at Beaux today to watch the drag brunch."

"Okay, I get it, Doc."

"So yeah, I want you gone, but it's not personal. I'm sure you need some time and space, too. You've been here all weekend."

"It's where I've wanted to be." I felt a sense of relief, though, to know Taylor was ditching me for a purpose. "But good to hear. You've got a booked and busy day ahead."

"That's my life," Taylor said. "It was like that before you. It'll stay that way until…we'll figure out everything. Working together on this accreditation project. Keeping things under wraps and professional on campus. Figuring out what's next, when the project is over and you're back in Chicago."

"Let's just keep it in the now for now, if that works for you," I said, kissing his hands. "Thanks for hearing me out."

"Thanks for hearing *me* out. We're in this together," he said. "Meet me at drag brunch later today. I'm sure Markell and the crew will be surprised to see us together."

"Together?"

"Yeah. We've got nothing to hide with our friends and family," he said. "Last time we were there, first time we met, we weren't in the best space together. When's the last time you talked with Manessa DelRey, by the way?"

"You have a point," I said. "You're doing the Lord's work encouraging me to reconnect with my family. Not promising anything, but it's a start."

"They don't call me Saint Taylor for nothing. I like you, Dustin. Yeah, we've had some good moments and some good sex, and we'll see where it goes. But I'm down to go down the road with you. We've got time. There's no rush."

That's what I needed to hear from Taylor. My nerves and anxiety quieted from five hundred to one hundred like that.

"I like you, too, Doc," I said. "A lot. More than I thought I would. But I'll stop right there before I start sounding—"

"You have nothing to worry about, so you can stop right

there." He leaned in to kiss me. "I'm the last person to pull a one and done on anyone. I ain't had nobody in a long time to one and done with, to be honest."

I heard my phone chime, signaling an incoming text. I excused myself and got up, feeling assured that my feelings for Taylor were reciprocated and matched mine. I went to the foyer bench and checked my phone, which had gone up to a respectable sixty percent during our morning talk.

"Well, perfect timing," I said as I scrolled through my phone and saw a current text message and many missed phone calls from the condo association president for my place in the Dogpatch neighborhood. "I need to get back to the hotel, change, get a workout in, and then go check up on something. Text me, and I'll meet you at Beaux later."

"Not so fast, Dustin," he said, grinning. He was definitely ready. Taylor walked over to me and gave me a hug. Also gave me a look I was learning to interpret as he was ready for another round.

"What are you trying to do to me, Doc?"

"Nothing," he said as he put his hands around my waist. "Just reassuring you that what I'm feeling is real."

I reached down to the front of Taylor's neon pink sweat shorts. The friction and warmth brought him to life down there once again.

"Oh, it's real, is it?" I traced Taylor's erection, which was forcing his shorts to tent in my direction. "It's definitely real."

"What are you doing to me, Dustin?"

"You know exactly what I'm doing." I winked an eye, put my hand in the elastic around his waist, and watched the shorts drop to the floor around his feet. I knelt in front of him. "I'm about to snatch your soul before the housecleaner gets here."

"Say less."

❖

Hours later, as promised, I sat at Markell's well at Beaux and waited on Taylor to show up. His event was running late, my errands had ended early, and we both had missed the drag brunch performances.

"We can do shots in a minute," Markell said to me as he walked around the somewhat empty bar. The brunch crowd and performers, including Manessa, had gone to other Sunday Funday spots in Castro. "Can you help me out a bit, though, Dustin? Skeletal crew of one, which means me, until the evening barbacks and bartenders arrive."

Markell showed me what to do. Pick up and put empty glasses on the back bar, where the evening barbacks would begin loading them into dishwashers behind the bar. Toss visible food in the green compost bins. Put all plastics in the blue recycling bins. Everything else in the trash. Any cash tips still lying around, hand directly to Markell. I'd never done bar or restaurant work, but I found it kinda refreshing rather than sitting behind a laptop or in another tedious meeting.

"Taylor said you do this bartending job, another one around the corner, and you're a personal trainer? I applaud you, bruh. How do you do it?"

Markell slid some remnants of nachos and half-eaten burritos into the compost bin and kept talking. "It's called rent in San Francisco. Unless you're in tech or pharmaceuticals or you're a consultant with a big firm, most of us out here working two or three jobs. Crazy, considering like sixty percent of SF residents got a comma and a couple degrees behind their names. Yours truly included. But you know this story. Your people in Oakland, right?"

"Bet." I took some empty glasses to the back bar. "But my

grandparents and their parents' generation came here because of the naval yards and shipbuilding back in the day. But that's another story."

"Ain't nobody Black-Black trying to move here anymore," Markell said. He was now behind the DJ booth, and put on our fave, *Renaissance*. "I was glad when Taylor moved up here from L.A. But I'm trying to get Nate, my husband, to maybe look elsewhere. Or if I get to strike out on my own and open my own bar. We'll see. Between my three jobs and his two teaching gigs at community colleges, it's too much sometimes not seeing each other on the regular except to sleep. I'm rambling, though. Shots? You doing Hennessy or tequila today?"

Between the two of us, we'd cleared up all the leftover brunch crowd items around the bar and were just waiting on Taylor to show up. I appreciated and valued the alone time with Markell. It was perfect for us to break the ice and feel each other out, especially where Taylor was concerned. Most of all, I knew it was important to make strides with the best friend of the man I was feeling.

"I can't do dark on an empty stomach, so tequila," I said as I sat at my spot at the bar and Markell returned to the well. "That dark fucked me up that first day I met you and Taylor. I was so hungover the next day. Thank goodness it was a three-day weekend."

Markell poured us a couple shots and adorned the glasses with little limes.

"Served you right," Markell said. "You were kind of an asshole that first day. I get it. I work at a bar. I see men all day who haven't mastered the art of the approach."

"I was. I apologize. I've apologized to Taylor multiple times."

Markell and I tapped our glasses on the bar top and downed our shots.

"Well, he's obviously forgiven you," Markell said. "I think he likes you, too. I *know* he likes you."

"I like him, too," I said. "We're taking it slow. No labels or anything yet."

"Oh, I know Taylor's not going fast. He's still weighing this whole 'I wanna be a campus president one day' thing when it comes to relationships. But you've gotten further with him than most I've known in a long time. Truth, there haven't been many. Well, any. Don't tell him I told you, Dustin."

"It's between us."

"You stay in Chicago, right?"

"For now."

"Any plans to move back to the Bay Area?"

"Hadn't really thought about it."

"Well, at some point, if y'all progress," Markell said, "y'all will need to have the talk about distance, monogamy, open, all that. Not that I'm in y'all business or anything."

"Are you and your husband?" I asked to deflect. I thought it might be some kind of test question to see where I stood on throuples. "Open?"

"Hell no. Physically, I could do it. People hit on bar staff all the time here, and I get a lot of offers that tempt me. Mentally, I'm not there. I'm a one man at a time man."

"Same here," I said. "And I'm not just saying that because you're Taylor's best friend. Though I'm not against being open. Whatever people decide together, I guess. I hope I get to meet Nate one day."

"We can do a spades night one of these days," Markell said. "And between you and me, this wasn't a test. I'm just making conversation until Taylor gets here. Sometimes I wonder why us gays get into relationships in SF, since half are open and involved in others' relationships. Anyway…"

Markell poured out another set of shots for us.

"I have no secrets to reveal, Markell." I put my hands up in front of me. "In case you're trying to get me to spill tea about me for Taylor."

Markell raised his shot glass. "No tea. This is to being Black-Black, being cool people, and being good for my bestie. And cheers to SF, love it or hate it."

Just as Markell and I downed the shots, definitely my last one, Taylor walked in. I was relieved. Again, his eyes lit up and his smile widened when he saw me sitting at the bar talking with Markell. That made me happy. I loved when he walked up behind me, hugged me, and kissed the back of my neck.

"Two of my favorites," Taylor said as he sat next to me. He grabbed one of my hands. "Sorry I'm late. The event went longer than expected. Glad to see you two are bonding. I miss anything?"

I leaned over and kissed Taylor. I missed him during the hours we'd been separated, though we'd spent most of the weekend together. We'd have to separate again soon, though, given that it was a work night and I'd be going back to my hotel up the street.

I separated my lips from Taylor's, and we smiled at each other.

"Just missed kissing you," I whispered. "I'll pull it together, Taylor. I know…slow."

We heard someone adjacent to us clearing their throat, and we turned around. Taylor's colleague Wes Jenkins breezed by us and beelined it to the bathroom in the back of the club. Or at least, it looked like Wes Jenkins.

"Yes, that was Wes Jenkins stumbling by," Markell said. "But he looked wasted. Very wasted. All the industry in Castro knows about Wes Jenkins and his Sunday Funday benders."

"Damn," Taylor said, standing up. "You think he saw us?"

"The way he stumbled by?" Markell said. "Nah. He's

wasted. Why don't the two of you get out of here now before he comes out. I can handle Wes Jenkins. Go on. Shots are on me, Dustin."

Taylor slid his hand in mine, and we nodded.

"Sounds like a plan," we said to each other, and to Markell, in unison. We walked hand in hand up Castro, then Eighteenth Street, until Taylor caught a rideshare in front of my hotel.

CHAPTER ELEVEN

Taylor

The campus president of the Cal U campus in Oakland resigned overnight. A news report alleged the campus had stockpiled dozens of sexual harassment and racial harassment cases with little or no follow-up. Even worse, the breaking news alleged that for years, the Cal U Oakland campus had failed to intervene in conflict-of-interest allegations, where high-level administrators engaged in conduct that put their ethics into question. As was the case with most high-profile news stories and college campuses, the university president took the fall.

"I'm going to be fucked," I whispered to myself as I made my way into the front doors of Merced Hall. Being dramatic, embodying anxiety, thinking too far into the future, and imagining something that hadn't quite happened. Classic me.

For days, I worried about Wes Jenkins and whether he'd seen Dustin and me together at Beaux or anywhere else outside of the campus setting embracing, kissing, or being closer than professional colleagues would or should be with each other. The idea of Wes Jenkins having anything over me to use as leverage in my professional life at the campus weighed on my mind. He already disliked me for whatever reasons that swirled in his mind.

The accreditation process was too important to the campus,

to President Weatherspoon, and to me. If anyone thought there was any kind of impropriety with the process because of my romantic involvement with the lead consultant, I imagined my job at Cal U Lake Merced would be over.

I knew that morning's news would make its way onto the president's cabinet meeting agenda later in the day. And it did.

"The chancellor's office called an emergency meeting of the CU presidents late last night when they knew this story would break," President Weatherspoon said as she started the weekly cabinet meeting with her updates and announcements.

I was liking her new pixie cut spiky wig that made her resemble Gladys Knight. But given the topics of today's meeting, I'd keep that compliment and thought to myself and not verbalize it. The cabinet consisted of all the university vice presidents serving as President Weatherspoon's inner circle of advisors. Serving on this leadership team was something I'd prepared for and taken seriously each week. It was definitely a blue suit, polished shoes, and nice tie day for me whenever we had this meeting.

"Effective immediately, all the veeps of human resources at each of the CU campuses will be sending out memos to campus employees reminding them of their mandatory reporting duties when it comes to sexual harassment and discrimination allegations," President Weatherspoon continued. "All employees will be expected to sign. The chancellor's office has asked us each to make sure our Title IX teams work in conjunction with the VPs of HR to ramp up progressive discipline processes with employees found responsible for repeat offenses or those involved in pending and future discrimination cases."

My peers got silent.

"Furthermore, presidents, vice presidents, and other high-level administrators will be under increased public scrutiny around conflicts of interest. Not only will I be talking with each of you one-on-one about any potential conflicts, but we're each going to have to re-sign our commitment to no conflicts of interest. That means we're all going to have to be above reproach, not that any of you haven't been as such."

Again, I thought, I'm going to be fucked.

I didn't know what Wes Jenkins knew about Dustin and me. And if he did, I didn't know when, if, or how he would use it against me. I had some thinking to do. Would it have been wise to self-disclose that I'd started a personal relationship with Dustin? Would it have been wise to keep quiet and say nothing until after the accreditation process ended, in hopes Wes Jenkins or anyone else wouldn't say anything? Would it have been wise to slow things down with Dustin? We had just another couple weeks of work together. What would it hurt to slow down even more?

Dustin and I'd already made a pledge to take things slow, though our sex life was anything but slow. After all, I'd gone a lifetime of *not* knowing Dustin. What would another few weeks of delay have meant? But what about my heart? My happiness? I hadn't allowed myself to think about those things for years until Dustin came along. Why let it change now?

At the same time, I wasn't a rule breaker. I didn't violate ethics. I'd always been known as the one who did everything above reproach. But now, I started thinking maybe crossing the line with Dustin and opening up my heart to him was the wrong decision. Maybe I should have just kept my focus on job, career, future campus presidency, as I'd always had. Why had I given in to Dustin's charm?

I snapped back to reality and to the present, emerging from my daydreaming, worrying, and carrying guilt, when President Weatherspoon called on me for the next agenda item in the meeting.

"Changing subjects, let's talk about an area that seems to be going really well for us," President Weatherspoon continued. "Dr. James, tell us how things are going with the accreditation teamwork you and Dr. McMillan are doing."

I gave my update. We had another week of accreditation meetings and interviews left before the process would wind down. Dustin and his team would then begin comparing their notes with what was in the initial self-assessment I'd pulled together. From there, Dustin would lead a final meeting for the campus community to hear what his team saw as our strengths, weaknesses, and opportunities looking forward. Then, weeks later, we would receive our official letter from Dustin and the Kane-Carlos Collective declaring us reaccredited or not reaccredited and for how long.

That evening, I made up an excuse to Dustin about needing to attend some late-night campus events. My calendar would soon be filling up with awards, banquets, and recognition ceremonies, culminating with graduation and commencement. Dustin would understand, I assumed. I needed a little time to think things through, and spending another night with Dustin wasn't going to help me.

"Hey Mom, hey Dad," I said as our faces appeared on the three-way Zoom call. I could see my dad was still in his office on campus at CU East L.A. My mom was in her office at home in Ladera Heights. I sat at my kitchen island, sipping on a glass of sparkling rosé while waiting on dinner delivery to arrive. "I need your advice."

I recapped my chance meeting with Dustin, how we hadn't hit it off initially, learning he was the lead consultant on the university accreditation process, and how we'd grown to appreciate and ultimately fall for each other while working together on the project.

"Fiona-Sheree doesn't know about you and the accreditation man, huh?" my mom asked. "Baby boy, you're in a tizzy."

It comforted and amused me my mom still called me a childhood nickname, though I was in my forties and she in her late sixties. Some habits never grew old.

"Especially with Eubanks's resignation," my dad chimed in. "I've been watching the news. I docusigned my ethics papers today. Eubanks has always been a good man in my book. He's helped generations of students get their degrees in the CU system."

"Baby boy, you need to tell her and HR right away," my mom said. "Woman's intuition. I bet Fiona-Sheree already has picked up on something between you two."

"We keep it one hundred professional at work," I said. I felt myself retreating into childhood mode, as if I was in trouble with my parents. Like I had something to hide, even though I wasn't really doing anything. "I promise. We don't talk work at all outside of work. Besides, he's a consultant, a contract worker, not even a campus employee."

"I think since you only got a week or so left of working together on the project, and no one knows anything already, you keep it to yourself," my dad said. "That's my two cents."

"Someone might know," I said. "Wes Jenkins. Though he hasn't said anything. Yet."

I saw my mom shake her head on camera.

"I get sick every time you mention his name, baby boy," my mom said. "Don't give Wes Jenkins something to hold over you. Title IX covers third party and contract workers in the CU system."

"I know."

"I read the handbook all the time to my new faculty," my mom said. "And let them know that any hint of a work relationship becoming more than that, to self-disclose it so that it doesn't come back to hurt them in terms of Title IX or other accusations. Tell Fiona-Sheree. And tell HR. I don't want this to backfire on your accreditation process and have people think you slept your way to a good campus report, baby boy."

"And I differ, respectfully, and I'm gonna be blunt," my dad said. "First, I agree with your mom for the most part. But what's that saying about people fucking in the workplace? *Above your level or below your level, leave it alone.* Not that it's right or wrong. You and this man are peers. He's not employed by the university. His firm is. I really think you're good. I ain't no attorney, though."

"You're a good boy," my mom said in a reassuring voice. "Always have been. I know you'll make the right decision. I just want you to stay focused on becoming a campus president. Jameses don't quit."

"I know, Mom," I said. "We don't quit. I still want to be a president. That's my next step, I know."

"You'll be our first campus president in the family, Taylor," my dad said. "Proud of you."

Making them proud had always been my priority. Same as they had been with their parents, so the stories they told me.

"Baby boy, I want you to be happy like Markell and Nate. I hope you find someone one day. You're not getting any younger, and your dad and I are getting older. We want to see you happy before we're gone. Now, I haven't asked you much about this Dustin man, but—"

"Does he make you happy?" my dad interrupted.

"Yes, he does."

"That's all that counts. You'll figure out the rest."

I couldn't remember the last time I'd even talked with my parents about someone I was interested in. "It's still early with Dustin, but I feel happy when I'm with him."

"Met any of his family yet?" my dad asked. "They come from the same stock as us?"

"Met his mom at her house in Oakland for dinner. That's another conversation for another day. Families are complicated."

I wished I'd been quiet about Dustin's mom. I regretted making any comments that might have come across as judgmental. Luckily, my parents didn't pick up on that.

"I can't wait to meet him," my mom said. "So, is this doubt you're feeling about him per se? Has he given you a reason to doubt him? Or is it about what you think other people are going to think if they find out you've been involved with this man? Or is it more about your career aspirations? There is a difference between the three—him, other people, or you. That's something to think about."

"Well, this is helpful," I said. "Why does life have to be so complicated? Can we go back to the days of you, me, and Markell with our cookies and listening to Sade in the dimly lit den?"

"It's a good question," she said. "I'm almost seventy. I've lived and seen some things. I miss those days, too. Y'all grow up too fast, baby boy."

Indeed, it was a good question.

I continued thinking long after our Zoom call ended. I sipped on another glass of rosé while I picked at the Pad Thai I'd ordered for dinner. It wasn't like me to have more than one drink on a worknight, though I knew lots of academics who were closet alcoholics, stressed from work, and could down a bottle or two of wine in one sitting at home after work. I didn't want to be one of those academics.

My phone chimed. A text from Dustin.

Hey doc. Thinking of you. Hope you're well. Good night :-)

I smiled at Dustin's text. It was nice to be thought of by someone for something other than fixing a crisis or responding to an ask or a want.

I texted him back a good night message.

I thought more about what my mom had asked. Was it Dustin, the thoughts of other people, or me?

Whatever it was, was it enough to get in the way of what I was feeling for him?

CHAPTER TWELVE

Dustin

"Penny for your thoughts," I said.

Taylor and I were alone in the conference room on the top floor of Merced Hall, where our accreditation work together had first begun weeks ago—that not-so-fun day when he was an hour late to the first meeting and I'd ripped into the sloppy report submitted by his team. It was the end of another workweek, our final week of interviews and meetings with campus constituents.

I'd just completed leading the capstone meeting with President Weatherspoon and much of her leadership team before many of them, except for Taylor, rushed off to an alumni fundraiser in downtown San Francisco, where the mayor would be the keynote speaker. I was glad for the alone time together in the conference room. Other than the meeting today, Taylor had been busy, or so he said, with planning work leading up to the university's graduation season, which was a few weeks away.

Taylor made himself busy around the room, straightening chairs, placing empty water bottles in the recycling bin, and turning off the large screen at the head of the room—work that administrative assistants and custodians were paid to do.

Clearly, he was avoiding me, not just today, but for the past several days.

"My thoughts are only worth a penny to you?" Taylor asked as he put clickers and remotes in their containers underneath the screen.

"Touché. I thought you'd be thrilled with the direction the accreditation process is going. I sang your praises and those of your team. But why was Wes Jenkins leading today's capstone meeting and not you? It's been that way for the past few days or so."

"I know," Taylor said as he avoided eye contact with me. "Thank you. I'm glad you see how hard we've been working to address the recommendations of the last accreditation work ten years ago."

Without saying it officially in the capstone meeting, I'd all but confirmed that Cal U Lake Merced would be reaccredited. Yes, my team still had work ahead writing up our findings and recommendations. But Taylor should have been on cloud nine.

"Is something up?" He hadn't answered my question about Wes Jenkins. I knew something was up, but I didn't know if I should press Taylor on it more or to let it chill. I thought we meant something to each other, where at least we'd talk if something were bothering us.

"No," Taylor said, forcing a fake yawn. "It's Friday. An end to a busy workweek. I'm tired."

I whispered, "We haven't seen each other all week, not even here on campus. Your text replies are not as quick as they once were, and when you do reply, they're one- or two-word responses. You've been busy, or so you say, with work events and we haven't hung out. You've sent Wes Jenkins, of all people, to sit in your place for meetings you should be attending with me. You didn't seem yourself today during the capstone meeting. And I gave you all a lot of good news."

"I know. I appreciate that. I'm glad accreditation is proceeding along well and that we're almost done."

Taylor breezed past me, his soap and cocoa butter wafting in the air, to gather his tablet, work bag, and suit jacket at the other end of the conference room. He was wearing the hell out of his tan suit pants, with his white polo shirt riding up perfectly in the back. If we weren't in the workplace, I'd have grabbed his ass and pulled him toward me. It had been too many days since he and I had been together.

"Bruh, for real. Is something up?" I asked. "Can we talk?"

"Not here," Taylor said. "Please?"

"Your place? I've missed you. I can't wait to get up next to you again."

"Not my place," Taylor said, continuing his hushed voice tone. "How about somewhere public today?"

"Public?" I was a little offended, considering all the private and alone time we'd spent at his apartment. "Are you for real, Doc?"

"You know what's going to happen if we go to my place," Taylor said, no feeling or emotion in his voice. "Probably not a good idea right now."

I was confused. Why had he been so distant lately? Why so suddenly? Why the hesitancy to be alone at his apartment? It hadn't been a problem before, especially once we'd started sleeping together. Obviously something was going on, but out of respect, I wasn't going to press or pressure him.

"All right." I put my hands up in surrender. "If you say so."

After he put on his suit jacket and before he left the conference room, he whispered, "Dinner. I'll text you an address and a time to meet."

❖

A couple hours later, I waited for Taylor at a small table on the back patio of Hot Johnnie's, a local restaurant specializing in pastrami sandwiches and other smoked meats. It was down the street from where I was staying at the Hotel Castro. Convenient, in case Taylor wanted to crash at my hotel after dinner. At least, I hoped he did. I missed my alone time with him.

I tried not to overthink Taylor's distant behavior the past few days, but I couldn't help it. How could someone go from hot to cold like that? Why was he so mysterious and peculiar in the conference room earlier? Had I done something that I didn't know about? I needed answers.

A server distracted me out of my thoughts and put down a set of silverware and napkins in front of me. I took a sip of bottled sparkling water I'd ordered and checked my phone for any notifications from Taylor. None. I glanced at a rerun of *RuPaul's Drag Race* that streamed on a TV monitor mounted nearby and adjacent to my table.

Taylor walked in looking casually chic in black denim jeans, a white T-shirt, black denim jacket, and Jordans. Seemed like the only times I'd seen Taylor were either in suits at work or naked in bed, so seeing him dressed fashionably and not looking like a college administrator was a nice surprise.

I got up to greet him. "It's giving 80s Michael Jackson. Looks good on you, Doc."

"Thanks."

I leaned in for a kiss, and he swerved his face so that I caught one of his cheeks instead.

"Okay."

"How are you, Dustin?" Taylor asked, giving me a closed-mouth smile. As he sat down, the server brought out my food order—a half pastrami sandwich and a small bag of waffle fries. "Yum, that looks good. Johnnie's food is really good."

"Oh yeah," I said, part question, part statement, and dipped a fry in a small container of ketchup. "What did you order?"

Taylor shook an index finger back and forth in the air.

"I'm not eating," he said. "At least not right now. I'll take a sip of your water, though, if you don't mind."

"For sure," I said, baffled. I handed the bottle to him. Something was definitely different with Taylor. With us. "So, why are we here if we're not eating together? Why'd you ask me to meet you at Hot Johnnie's for dinner?"

Taylor took an invitation out from his jacket pocket and slid it across the table to me.

"I'm going to a party across the street at the Mix," Taylor said with another closed-mouth smile. "They're closing down for a couple hours for the staff at Beaux to have a private staff party. I forgot about it until Markell reminded me today after work."

I read the invitation. A pre-summer, pre-Pride staff appreciation event. All the bartenders, barbacks, drag performers, and select customers invited for open bar, heavy appetizers, and karaoke.

"This looks fun, Doc," I said as I handed the invitation back to Taylor. "Can I be your plus-one?"

Taylor made a face and shrugged his shoulders. "I hadn't planned on it," he said. "I mean, I'm Markell's plus-one, since Nate is teaching night classes. I can ask, though."

Oh, he could ask? Something was up, I continued to think.

"Nah, it's okay," I said. "I can take my food to go and walk back to my hotel. I'm tired anyway."

"I can text Markell," Taylor said.

"It's no big deal."

We stared at each other for a few seconds until I broke the silence.

"Are we good?" I asked. "Because I'm starting to have this feeling something's going on."

Taylor put his hands across the table and reached for mine. Just as I'd been thinking. I knew this wouldn't be good.

"President Weatherspoon knows about us," he said. "At least, I'm pretty sure she does."

I took my hands away from his, stood up, and paced around the patio near our table a little bit.

"What? How?"

Taylor explained that he sought his parents' advice about his involvement with me after the President Eubanks resignation incident. After consulting with his parents, he said he'd decided not to say anything to anyone at the university, but President Weatherspoon had called him into her office, given him a directive to fill in for some of her meetings for the week, taken him off the accreditation project, and put Wes Jenkins in his place.

"I think President Weatherspoon reassigned me to some of her work this week in order to save me professionally, in a way," Taylor said. "So there'd be no conflict of interest by me being with you and you leading the accreditation team's work."

I sat back down.

"But how did she find out?" I asked. "Wes Jenkins?"

"No," Taylor said. "My mom, I'm pretty sure of it. You know moms. Even if you tell them something's a secret or not to share with anyone. Probably...no, she did...went into tiger mom mode and called up President Weatherspoon. They go way back professionally and personally. They were on the same line back in the day."

Still, I was confused. Why the cold shoulder and distance all week? "You couldn't tell me?" I asked. "I thought we were beginning to mean something to each other."

Taylor sighed. "Dustin, I know when I've been given another chance. I've had a pretty easy and lucky life. I wasn't going to mess it up."

"And?"

"So, I did what I needed to do, and that meant playing the role and distancing myself from you and the accreditation project," Taylor said.

"It makes sense, but it also doesn't make sense." I scrunched up my face, feeling and showing confusion for Taylor's logic. I mean, I thought we had genuine feelings developing between us.

Taylor was starting to look annoyed at me for starting to look annoyed at him. "Feelings are there. You're making a deal out of nothing."

"I'm confused, Doc."

"I'm not compromising or inconveniencing my career aspirations. I want to be a campus president. I know President Weatherspoon is and was trying to save me and my career."

I couldn't believe what I was hearing from Taylor. I paused and took a sip of water before I continued.

"So, you're saying I'm a compromise? An inconvenience to *your* career goals?"

Taylor's eyes widened. "Oh my gosh, I'm sorry, Dustin. I didn't mean it like—"

At that moment, I felt a tap, well, more like a massage, on my shoulders. I turned around. Silas. My ex.

"I thought that was you," Silas said. His eye contact, with his piercing green eyes, was mesmerizing, penetrating. "What's up, Dustin? Long time."

He moved to my side and I got a longer look at him in his standard wardrobe—a white tank top, despite the chilly San Francisco nighttime air outside, and freeballing in light gray basketball shorts. I could see the outline and head of his penis, which I'd had fond memories of before discovering he was voting for Republicans. He carried a duffel bag, which I knew was for his change of clothes as a go-go dancer. His waves and fade were immaculate and fresh as always. The perks of being twenty-nine and fine. That was Silas.

"What's up, Silas? What brings you by?"

I should have introduced Taylor to Silas, but given that I was pissed off at Taylor at the moment, I decided to let introductions wait a bit. Show a little petty. I thought back to how it unnerved Taylor at the retreat cottage when I shouted out Silas's name. I wondered if Taylor was unnerved now.

"You, with your sexy ass," Silas said. He squinted and nodded at me. Sucked on his bottom lip a bit, too. Without an invitation to do so, he sat down across from me next to Taylor. By now, I should have introduced them, but I wanted to play reindeer games for a bit. Taylor'd really hurt my feelings. "I'm dancing at Midnight Sun tonight. Just came by to pick up a little something to snack on from Johnnie's. Didn't know I'd maybe pick up a little Dustin, too."

Silas smiled. I smiled. Taylor looked around, like neither Silas nor me was there.

"We not like that anymore, Silas. You know better."

"Your mom still think we like that. How is that beautiful mom of yours doing, by the way?"

"You still visit her, you should know," I said, knowing I needed to introduce Taylor and Silas. "Silas, this is Taylor. Taylor, Silas my ex. Who needs to act more like an ex."

Taylor looked Silas up and down and nodded at him. Silas grinned at Taylor.

"Just a little convenient pandemic relationship," he said. "Till outside opened up and Dustin got on the first plane to Chicago and never looked back—till now, I guess."

"It ended long before outside opened up," I said. "And you know why. Voting for Forty-Five's ass."

"Wait a minute," Silas said. "Is this the little straitlaced saintly one who gets all the girls and queens into college? Finally, a name to a face. Thank you for your service to the community, bitch."

Taylor gave a quick closed-mouth smile.

Silas continued. "By day, I'm a high school gym teacher and dance coach over in Bayview-Hunters Point. We need to stay in touch. I want to get more of my students to apply to the Lake Merced campu—"

"I'm glad you got picked up again by the school district," I interrupted. Didn't want Silas finding any way to forge a connection with Taylor. Didn't want more worlds colliding. "Maybe you can start paying rent and condo association fees again. The company keeps texting and calling me about—"

"Maybe you can let me pay you in other ways."

I broke in, again, before things went south.

"Silas, Taylor and I are seeing each other. We have been since I've been back in town."

"Oh, that's right. The Lake Merced campus project. How cute. Professional colleagues and fuck buddies."

Taylor cleared his throat. "Well, I'm late for the party," he said, and stood up. "We can talk later, Dustin."

"Doc…"

"Hey, saint, you don't have to leave on my account," Silas said to Taylor, winking at me. "I'm picking up my food and heading next door to Midnight Sun. Y'all should come see me dance later. Tip me some twenties so I can make enough to catch up on the rent I owe you, Dustin."

Silas laughed and smiled. He was still as charming and funny as I'd remembered. I tried not to get distracted by his swinging penis in his basketball shorts as he stood up next to Taylor.

"I do appreciate you letting me keep your place over in Dogpatch, though," Silas said. "Especially how things went down after you stopped going down."

"I'll explain later, Taylor."

"Don't worry about it," Taylor said. "Good meeting you, Silas. Good to put a face to a name, too."

Silas bumped fists with Taylor and then looked at Taylor and me.

"Look at you two," Silas said. "Same height. Same build. Same haircut. Same look. It's like twincest or something. If you all need a third to break up the monotony…"

Silas hugged me and ground his dick into my hip before leaving.

"No thirds," I said out loud to Silas as he left the patio toward the front part of the restaurant. "No thanks."

Taylor and I stared at each other. We still weren't resolved about "compromise" and "inconvenience." And I'm sure he had a million questions about Silas, me, and what might have appeared to be chemistry between us.

However, the words didn't come. I wondered if they'd ever come.

CHAPTER THIRTEEN

Taylor

I was pissed off at Dustin and darted as fast as I could across the street from Hot Johnnie's to the Mix.

I took the complimentary gelatin shot one of the hosts offered at the door, and went to the end of the front bar, where Markell was ordering drinks. It was a staff appreciation event for the Beaux employees and invited guests, so there was open bar for an hour and a half, and that night I planned to partake of more than one drink. Especially with how heated I was feeling. I'd have the weekend to recover if I needed to.

"I got you, Taylor." Markell handed me a shot of tequila and a double-sized Cadillac margarita. "Cheers."

"I needed that," I said. "And I might take another one before we leave."

Though it was a packed venue, with all of Markell's coworkers and friends, we'd found room at the end of a table on the back patio. Even ran into my student assistant Justin Monroe, who apparently was dating one of the Beaux go-go dancers and had gotten invited. After Markell introduced me to some of the people he worked with who were sitting at our table, I unloaded.

"Did you know that Dustin's ex, Silas, is the porn star

'The Silas Touch'?" I asked Markell, while putting air quotes up.

"*That* Silas is his ex? The one Dustin and Manessa DelRey were arguing about…something about a refrigerator that day you and Dustin met at Beaux? He used to go-go dance for us. That one?"

"Yeah, that one."

"I'm confused, Taylor," Markell said. "One, how do you know it's his ex? And two, how do you know he's who you say he is?"

"One, because I just met him. Dustin and I were just at Hot Johnnie's and that was a hot mess," I said. "And two, I know because I'm a fan, and I subscribe to *The Silas Touch* fan page."

"You subscribe?" Markell asked, his mouth ajar. "O-M-G. I never would have imagined."

"I don't date, I work, so I subscribe," I said. "Sex positivity. Everyone watches porn these days."

"And everyone in Castro knows someone who does porn, no biggie."

"And that's fine," I said. "I just didn't know I was watching and getting off to Dustin's ex. I am so pissed."

I slammed my open hand on the table. It shook my and everyone else's drinks.

"Why? What happened?"

"Where to freaking begin, I don't know," I said. "First, Mom has a big mouth. You know this already, though. It impacted me at work, and I put a chill on Dustin and me working so close together for a few days. He didn't like it. I met him across the street to explain it, and I said some pretty insensitive stuff that I didn't think was insensitive right away, but I tried to apologize. And then Silas happens to stop at

Johnnie's before his dancing gig at Midnight Sun, and at first, I was like, 'Damn, he fine and got a big dick,' then, 'Damn, that's the porn guy The Silas Touch,' and then I was like, 'Why is The Silas Touch all over my Dustin like that' in my head."

"What?" Markell asked, mouth still ajar as he took in more of my story.

"So, they're sitting there in front of me flirting and talking and reminiscing, like I wasn't there and like it was *their* date," I said, banging on the table again. "And then more fucking secrets. Always withholding something. He's not a liar. But he's not forthcoming. He withholds important details as if he thinks someone's gonna hold it against him."

"What do you mean?"

"Well, let's go back to day one and his name, I mean names."

"Okay, that."

"I mean we all have exes—well, not me," I said. "But you'd think Dustin would tell me his most recent ex is a porn star. Got me feeling all paranoid now about how good I am or not good in bed."

"If you were bad, he wouldn't keep you around. Trust, I know how the world turns in Castro."

"And you'd also think Dustin would tell me he still has a place here in the city in the Dogpatch neighborhood," I said. The two shots and the strong Cadillac margarita were getting to me. "I'm buzzing and rambling, I know. I'm sorry, Markell. This is your work party. We should be mingling."

"I'm following along, Taylor," Markell said. "So, why the hell is he staying in the Hotel Castro, if he has a place already in the city?"

"Exactly," I said. "As much shit as Dustin talked about San Francisco that first day he showed up at Beaux, you mean to tell me he'd lived here long enough to either rent, buy, or keep a place? Bad enough he withheld that he grew up in Oakland. Oh, but it gets better."

"What?"

"I'm just piecing this together, mind you. Dustin and I haven't talked about any of these fucking secrets." I grabbed a gelatin shot off the tray being passed around the table. I sucked it down quickly, leaving no remnants. "So, apparently Dustin and Silas lived together through the pandemic. I still don't know how they met, nothing. Then something about Silas voting for Forty-Five."

"If I'm remembering correctly,, Silas is one of those mixed Black boys who didn't grow up around Black people, allegedly."

"Whatever to that, no excuse," I said. "I don't care for no Black Republicans either, so I gotta wonder about Dustin's judgment there. So, anyway, they break up and Dustin moved to Chicago, but here's the kicker. Apparently, he left and is letting Silas stay in his place in Dogpatch. And from the sound of it, Silas ain't paying rent or condo fees regularly. So, Dustin is footing the bill for his freaking ex to have a place to live in SF."

"Get the fuck out."

"Wait, there's more," I said as Jonathan, one of Markell's bartender colleagues, slid a couple more tequila shots to us. We tapped glasses and took the shots. "And I'm already pissed off, but this part here pissed me off even more. Dustin and Silas have been in communication with each other."

"Well, that makes sense," Markell said. "I mean, they have the whole Dogpatch place and rent thing going."

"Nah. How did Silas know about Dustin and me working together on the accreditation process at the university? And he knew about me getting Manessa, Coco Hydrate, and others into college."

"Well, damn," Markell said. "They talk. But I mean, the service industry is a small profession. Everyone who works in Castro knows everyone who works here."

"Yeah, they talk all right," I said. "About a little too much, if you ask me. But whatever. I've never had a boyfriend or an ex. What do exes have to talk about together?"

"One day. Some day. You'll know."

"Well, Dustin ain't my boyfriend, but he's about to get the ex-factor treatment," I said. "This is what I get for not staying focused on my one goal."

"We all know you want to be a university president," Markell said, like clockwork, like an anthem he's heard over and over. "The first Black, openly gay, and relatively young university president in the U.S."

"And I'm not letting that goal slip through my hands for a relationship. I'm not hurting my career for Dustin. Fuck that."

"You *are* heated," Markell said. "Let's bring it down a notch or two. You said earlier you told him some insensitive things. What did you say?"

"Fuck," I said. "I can't believe what came out of my mouth."

"What was it?"

"I implied he was an inconvenience to my career goals," I said. "That he was making me compromise my dreams."

"Ouch, Taylor," Markell said. "That's bad."

"I know."

"So, what now?" Markell said. "What about you and Dustin?"

"Well, I *am* going to apologize to him," I said. "I don't deserve for it to be accepted, because that was pretty low for me. I don't say or think those kinda things."

"But you did say those kinda things to Dustin," Markell said. "What about what's next?"

"I don't wanna get hurt," I said. "As much as I care for Dustin, and that's a lot for me to say since I don't let *anybody* in romantically, I think I wanna slow it down. He's going back to Chicago in a week or so anyway, and I don't think he's planning to be back in the Bay Area anytime soon. I mostly don't wanna get hurt."

"Like hurt as in inconvenience or compromise to your career goals?"

I paused and looked at Markell. If he hadn't gone the hospitality management route in college, I swear he'd have been a great therapist. In a way, that was what he did on the daily in his various jobs at the gay bars and at the gym—listen to people and their problems while doing his own work.

"Maybe I'm not so nice after all."

"Taylor," Markell said. "You're nice. You're the nicest person I know. You're a saint in the eyes of so many people, including many of my coworkers here."

"Thanks."

"But you don't have to be a saint," Markell said. "All you have to do is be human. Be real. Be you. Be yourself."

Though I was slightly buzzed, Markell's words brought me back to earth. Grounded me.

"Thanks for listening," I said. "I needed to vent and to hear what you just said."

"That's what best friends who are like brothers are for," Markell said. "You need to go find him, apologize to him, and talk to him. Tonight. If you can."

I pulled out my phone and crafted a short text to Dustin: *I'm sorry, Dustin. I'm still in Castro if you want to talk.* I hit send and turned the screen over.

"Okay, there," I said. "We'll see what happens."

"Good," Markell said. "Because...well, I know we're all in our forties and somewhat mature, but Silas ain't. You don't want Dustin walking around in Castro sad, mad, maybe drinking, because of a misunderstanding. You don't want Silas sniffing around a sad or mad Dustin, especially with his hotel just up the street."

"Damn, I didn't even think about that, Markell. Fuck, what if I push them back together. Even if just for one night. I mean, Silas is sexy. He could talk a priest out of his liturgical clothes."

"Oh, I bet he could."

"You think that'll happen? Dustin and Silas."

"I'm a bartender," he said. "I've seen people ruin the best relationships because of a spontaneously bad decision due to a temporary disappointment and drinking too much. Not that Dustin's gonna do it or you're gonna push him to it, for that matter. I'm glad you reached out to him. Maybe you should chill on the shots and drinks. You're more of a lightweight than you think."

I felt my phone vibrate on the table and I turned it over. A text from Dustin: *I'm in the Lobby Bar.*

CHAPTER FOURTEEN

Dustin

The folk acoustic sound of Tracy Chapman's song "The Promise" playing in the background at the Lobby Bar was nice and soothing. It was a welcome contrast to all the oontz-oontz-oontz music blasting from the clubs that I passed while taking the long route through Castro and walking back to my hotel. The alone time sauntering through the neighborhood, plus a nightcap, was what I needed after what went down between Taylor and me at Hot Johnnie's.

I sat solo at a corner table in the dimly lit bar. I loved the ambience—the rich, forest green patterned walls, the matching plush velvety seats, and the gold-colored lighting fixtures and candle holders. I took a sip of the Hennessy neat I'd ordered. I felt Taylor's presence. I looked up and motioned for him to take a seat.

"I'm glad you returned my text," Taylor said hesitantly, sitting across from me. "For a second, I didn't think you would."

I was surprised he'd reached out to me so quickly. Thought for sure a couple days would pass before speaking with each other again. I could smell tequila on his breath and slid my water glass to him.

"Of course I was gonna text you back, Taylor," I said. "We're too old to be playing relationship games and giving the silent treatment."

"So, now I'm Taylor again? No more Doc?" he asked with a hint of a slur in his voice, and he shrugged. "That's fair, I guess."

He downed the water quickly, and intuitively, the server brought over two more waters to our table. Before I'd started hanging out, dating, and sleeping with Taylor, I'd come to the Lobby Bar after work at the university for a happy hour drink, or come downstairs from my room for a nightcap after doing some work. Being a hotel guest and a regular, so to speak, the staff knew me well and were extra attentive.

"How was the party?" I asked. "You sound and smell like you had a good time and a few drinks."

"It was fun being with Markell and the Beaux staff. Sat and talked with Markell most of the time. And yeah, I had a few shots and a couple tall margaritas."

"I can tell."

"I'm sure I'll pay for it tomorrow," he said. "Lucky it's the weekend. Recovery time."

"Recovery is a good thing," I said. "So is reflection."

I was wondering when we'd get to the elephant in the room. The reason I returned his text. The reason I let him know where I was. The reason he walked up the street from the Mix to meet me at the Lobby Bar.

"I guess we're both a little mad at each other," Taylor said, breaking the silence. "Rightly so."

I took a sip of my drink.

"Oh, more than rightly so, I'd say."

"That's fair."

"So, I've been reflecting, and here's what I'll take responsibility for, Taylor," I said. "Big picture, I know I come across as someone who's not always honest, or let's say not forthcoming, when it comes to sharing who I am. I own that."

"You took the words out of my mouth, Dustin," Taylor said. "Dishonesty and lies of omission. I feel like with you, every day it's like 'what else?' and it makes me feel uneasy about you."

"No excuse, but we've only known each other a few months—weeks, when you get down to it," I said. "How long have we been living our lives and not knowing each other? Again, not an excuse, but we will always be learning something new about each other."

"That's fair."

"Now, Silas," I said. "He's a bit much, I know. I can imagine how upset you were with not only how you met Silas, and believe me that was not planned at all since you picked the restaurant, but upset at how he and I interacted with each other."

"I was a little bit—no, I was a lotta bit heated," he said. "Your ex is fine, younger than us, charming, flirtatious, does porn, blah blah blah. All the things I'm not. I am still sitting with the obvious chemistry between you two, even though I gather it was mostly a pandemic relationship. I mean, I can be jealous and move on, knowing you like me, knowing you and I are developing something."

"You ain't gotta worry about Silas that way at all," I said. "He don't know his shelf life is waning. For me and him, it was good while it lasted, but it's history. I'd never disrespect you that way, but I do own being petty for taking my time introducing you two. That part was disrespectful."

"Thanks."

"And for the record, yeah, I kept my place in the city since I left after the pandemic." I took another sip of my drink. "I've let him stay there since I moved away, and it's been a financial mess for me. I'm trying to get caught up on the mortgage and taxes because he owes me rent and condo fees, and I'm trying to get disentangled from all that. The trials and tribulations of forties life—we need to teach the baby gays."

"Let me know if I can help in any way."

"You're too kind, Taylor," I said. "You work in higher education. I know what kind of money you make and don't make. You can't afford to help the condo situation."

"Dustin, I got it. Whatever you need. Don't worry."

"You and your parents' third-generation college-going deep pockets. I hate that my family got the bad genes when it comes to money and money management. I'm trying to change that. You ain't gotta think about nothing. Probably never have."

"I can't help what I have and how I grew up," he said. "But anyway, whatever you need."

"I'll figure it out, thanks," I said. "I always find myself being everybody's ATM in some way. I'm working on it. That and the lies of omission part. Carrying shame about who and where I came from. Trying so obnoxiously to be someone's number one to make up for feeling like number two growing up. I got work to do on myself."

Taylor smiled at me and reached out for my empty hand, which I let him hold since we hadn't touched in a while. Felt good for the moment.

"If this is how we argue and fight," Taylor said, "then I can't wait to see how we make up."

I pulled my hand back. I took a deep breath. I know he hadn't thought we were done with only me taking responsibility for my behaviors.

"We're not having a knock-down drag-out because we're in an intimate spot like this in front of mixed company." At most there was room for fifteen to twenty people in the bar. There were maybe six other non-Black people scattered about.

No way was I planning to raise my voice in public. "But what about you? What do you own, Taylor?"

"You can call me Doc again," he said. "We're definitely not strangers or acquaintances or just colleagues working on a project anymore."

"True. But anything you own? Anything you take responsibility for?"

"Definitely. I should have told you about why the disappearing act and pretending to pull away from you. That it was self-preservation for me in terms of my career and an act of protection in terms of you and your work with my campus."

"I hear you," I said. "I think I would have understood. Or at least would have tried to make sense of it. If you had said that. But anyway, go on."

"I own that I could and should have trusted you more," he said. "I mean, you told me you make presidents. I should have known you'd understand and always have my back."

I signaled to the server that I was ready for the bill, which I was just going to sign and charge to my room.

"Okay, I guess that's it, then," I said. "These past couple hours I've been sitting with something you said and I can't get it out of my head. Compromise and inconvenience."

Taylor looked down, as if embarrassed, then looked at me again. He reached for my hands across the table.

"I apologize for saying that to you, Dustin. I am usually very thoughtful and measured with what I say. But I never meant to say or imply that you're those words to me. If anything, it was more about the temporary situation with the conflict of interest, the temporary reassignment from President Weatherspoon, and... Let me stop. I was wrong. I never should have said those words in relation to you or me. Especially knowing how they might connect to your feelings about how you grew up. I own that."

The server brought over the bill. I released my hands from Taylor's to sign it quickly and returned it back to the server.

"I'ma be honest with you, Taylor," I said. "I like you. I *really* liked you up until that moment."

"Liked?"

"All along during this accreditation work project, I kept telling myself to hold back, don't catch feelings, pull back, not pursue anything with you," I said. "Mostly because we were working together on this assignment, I respected you, and I didn't want to do anything to get in the way of your career goals. If only you were privy to the conversations in my head."

"I'm listening."

"But I decided to give in, pursue, and go for it," I said. "I told myself someone like you rarely comes along. Black. Attracted to Black people, especially in a place like San Francisco. Intelligent. Focused. Kindhearted. Close to me in age and life experience. Going somewhere. And someone I wanted to go somewhere with."

"Wanted?" Taylor asked. "Why are you speaking in past tense? We're here. Right now. I was hoping we would go upstairs to your room and make up. Can't believe I haven't even seen your hotel room."

"Doc, stop. Listen."

"Okay."

"Whether you meant to imply it or not, the words you said—'compromise' and 'inconvenience'—hurt me," I said. "A lot."

"That wasn't my intention."

"They cut like a knife," I said. "For the past couple hours, I've been sitting with those words. I walked around Castro to calm myself down."

"I was heated, too," he said. "But go on."

"I almost stopped by to see Silas dance at Midnight Sun. But I didn't."

"You did? You still got feelings for him?"

"Hell nah. Revenge sex ain't mature. Not for me."

"Well, I guess I appreciate your honesty there."

"I know I need therapy," I said. "What you said took me back to feelings I don't want to remember about growing up with my mom, my brother, my family. Feeling like I was in the way for a lot of reasons. Feeling like I was convenient to them when they need something from me, but otherwise get the fuck on. It's too much to explain, and you're not a psychologist, so I'll stop."

"I'm really sorry, Dustin," Taylor said. "I don't think you're a compromise or inconvenience to me. I didn't mean to imply that. Or trigger memories."

"Thanks," I said. "I have a lot of work to do on myself in terms of what I carry with my family situation and how I grew up. I probably don't...I shouldn't...I don't deserve love at this point in my life. Especially from someone like you, with all you've come from and all you've got going for you. I've come to realize we're just different, and it was a mistake to fall for you."

Taylor reached out and grabbed my hands again. To be considerate, I didn't pull away.

"All this from tonight? Just this night?"

I took a deep breath again.

"I shouldn't have let my guard down," I said. "Should have kept it platonic and professional once we figured out we'd be working together. I crossed a line, and I never should have put you in that situation."

"So, what are you saying, Dustin?"

Our eyes met and held. I think he knew.

"I'm going to chill on my feelings," I said. It felt like a movie. I couldn't believe I was saying what I was saying, especially how hard, fast, and relentlessly I'd pursued Taylor since meeting him. "I have a life back in Chicago. I can finish the rest of the accreditation report follow-up work over there."

"Chill on your feelings? Does that mean chill on us?"

The server interrupted, ironically, and called out to the few people sitting in the bar, "Kitchen and bar are about to close down. It's the last call."

Taylor and I stared at each other. The server began their bar closing duties, wiping down tables, straightening up chairs and barstools, and picking up bowls with leftover mixed nuts. The few remaining bar patrons signed their bills and gathered their things to leave. We pulled our hands apart and followed suit to the front sidewalk outside the bar. It had gotten much chillier and there was steam coming from our mouths as we breathed and talked.

"Yes," I said as we stood by a wooden bench underneath a street light. "That's what it means. I don't think we should do this anymore. I'm flying out to Chicago in the morning. I tried to get an overnight flight tonight, but it's too late."

Taylor reached out to me, and I stepped back.

"Dustin," he said. "You're mad at me. I don't think this is insurmountable. We can work this out."

"Come on, bruh," I said. "No scenes. No begging. I'm not mad at you. I mean, I was. But I got over it as we talked. I hear where you're coming from in terms of your job and career. I can't fault you for that."

Taylor started to tear up. Fuck, don't do this, I thought, as I held my own tears in. Crying in front of dates, boyfriends, exes, whatever, was a no-no for me.

"I have feelings for you, Dustin, believe it or not," he

said. "I mean, I don't want to say love, but I definitely have feelings."

"I caught feelings, too," I said. I needed to stay strong in my decision and resolve. "I'm just telling you what *I* want to do right now. I want to chill. I want us to chill. Please just respect that."

We stared at each other. A teardrop fell from the corner of one of Taylor's eyes and rolled slowly down his cheek. I wanted to catch and dry it, but I was on the verge of my own tears flowing, and I knew touching him would spark emotions I didn't want to feel or express at the moment.

"All right," he said as he pulled out his phone. "If that's how it is. I'll just call for a car to take me home. I'm sorry."

"I'll wait for you while—"

"No, don't," he said. "Waiting with you out here will only make me feel regret for how this night turned out. I don't want that. I just want to go to my apartment."

"You're still buzzed. I don't want anything to happen to you. I can wait."

"You should go upstairs to your room and *chill*, Dustin," he said. "I'll be okay out here for three minutes. And everyone's walking home from the clubs now. It's safe. I'll be fine."

"Fine." I turned to head toward the hotel entrance again. I pulled out my phone and pressed it against the keypad near the door, but before entering the door, I turned around and said, "Let me know when you get home, then. At least do that."

As I went inside and headed toward the stairwell, I wondered if that night would be the last time I'd see Taylor and if I'd regret my decision to have us slow down.

CHAPTER FIFTEEN

Taylor

Is it really a breakup if you really weren't together?

That was a question in my mind over the next three weeks, as I immersed myself in work and tried to stop thinking about Dustin, who made good on his promise to leave San Francisco for Chicago and finish the accreditation report remotely. So that I wouldn't have to repeat the story multiple times, I wrote, copied, and texted the same message to Markell and Nate, my mom and dad, and Miss Coco Hydrate and Manessa DelRey: *Dustin and I are through. Don't ask about it. It's the end-of-year on campus. I'm busy. I'm fine.*

That was enough of an explanation, as far as I was concerned.

We had glided into what was one of the busiest and most festive times of the academic year at California University Lake Merced, when everyone's attention on campus focused on ending the school year. It was convenient for me to stay on campus morning, noon, and night.

Not only did I have my regular roster of back-to-back meetings and a to-do list to get through in the day, I attended student organization awards banquets. I gave remarks at leadership and recognition ceremonies. I handed out certificates and shook hands with students and their supporters. I smiled with students and families when they asked me, a campus vice president, to pose in group photos, whether they knew me or not.

The smiles at campus celebrations, though genuine in the moment, faded away at the end of each workday when I'd get home and start to think of Dustin. Alone, each night, I'd eat dinner and drink one glass of wine while trying to put him out of my mind.

I found myself listening to music that mirrored whatever feelings came up. Some nights, I'd put on repeat a song like Whitney Houston's "Run to You," where she sang of acting in control all day yet coming home alone to an empty house at night. Or I'd sing along to Frank Ocean's "Thinkin Bout You," and wonder if Dustin was thinking of me at that moment or ever. Others, I'd put on a song that echoed rage at a partner and confidence in moving on like Beyoncé's "Sorry." Most of the time, I'd ask Alexa to find a playlist of heartache and breakup songs that included a little bit of Toni Braxton, Jazmine Sullivan, Sade, Summer Walker, Linda Martell, and Mariah Carey, minus the Mariah Carey wall sliding moments. On my most angst-filled and dramatic nights, anything by Dame Shirley Bassey.

On more than one occasion, an email from Dustin would show up in my work inbox. I'd get excited initially when I saw his name, until I saw the subject line, which was always one word—accreditation—and with a request for something he needed, with reminders of how quickly he wanted a reply from me. I complied with all his requests—whatever and whenever he wanted.

Dustin needed clarification on the English department's learning outcomes and how the faculty measured student success. Found it. Dustin needed to know how we were tracking retention and graduation rates of transgender and genderqueer students. It was my pet project, so I sent what I thought I'd made clear during his in-person campus interviews when he was in San Francisco. Dustin needed to know how President Weatherspoon and I had decided who would be on the Cal U Lake Merced accreditation team and what was the rationale. Since President Weatherspoon and I were in sync on all things related to campus, I responded with our strategy for identifying the who, what, and why of the team we'd assembled, including why I was chosen to chair the campus efforts. Each response back to me was punctuated with a blunt, "Received. No further explanation or information needed at this time."

All Dustin's email requests told me he was keeping his word of continuing the accreditation work remotely, that he was keeping it a hundred percent professional between us, that he wasn't trying to have any other contact with me beyond the report, and that he was trying to wrap up the project. It felt cold.

It made me sad. Especially after all we'd shared in the weeks he was in San Francisco. It went from him pursuing me while I resisted, to me giving in and taking a chance on love. Though I hadn't planned on falling for Dustin, I did. He meant something to me for me to put aside my line in the sand about career.

It also made me angry.

Angry at myself, primarily, for letting Dustin in when initially I hadn't liked him. Angry at myself for getting distracted by a relationship when all along I knew romance was not what I pictured or wanted in my life. Angry for catching feelings for Dustin, for not texting him that night after the discussion-argument we had at the hotel bar, and for feeling conflicted in the moment. Angry at myself and wondering how I could have fallen for someone I barely knew, whom I'd gone all my life without knowing, who was just a blip on the timeline of my life.

Being angry was an easy way to minimize any feelings I'd had for Dustin. It made it easier to accept that we were through, though we'd never really officially been a thing.

Just then, the apartment doorbell rang. I wasn't expecting anyone, not even food delivery. Could Dustin have flown back from Chicago, changed his mind about working remotely, and wanted to start us over? Would he have done this without messaging me?

I opened the door. No. It wasn't Dustin.

"We were wondering if you were still alive," Markell said as he and Manessa DelRey entered my apartment and breezed right by me. Markell was pulling Manessa's neon pink roller bag they used to carry their gowns and wigs on performance days at Beaux or other clubs in the Castro. "It's been four Sundays, at *least*, since you've been to drag brunch."

"And as many weeks since you've led the group at the LGBTQ Center," Manessa said with their trademark tongue pop. They looked stunning with their street clothes, no wig, and no performing makeup. "Bitches been missing you."

"Thank goodness I remembered the code to get into your building," Markell said. He set Manessa's bag in the front foyer, near the bench where Dustin and I first… "The parentals begged me to stop by and check in on you after I finished work."

I shut the door behind them. Had it really been that long since I'd been off the radar with Markell and Manessa? With my volunteer duties? With my parents? I know I'd checked in with my mom and dad, though they were busy with their own end-of-academic-year activities in L.A.

"To what do I owe this visiting the sick and shut-in Sunday

occasion to?" I asked. "Did we have plans or something?" Surely, I would have remembered.

"You do now," Manessa said. Tongue pop. They sat a large brown bag on the kitchen island counter. Definitely food. Smelled delicious. "Dinner and streaming the latest *Drag Race* episode."

"And making sure you're okay," Markell said. "We all know about you and Dustin."

"That dumbass cousin of mine," Manessa said. "But anyway."

"I'm fine," I lied. "It's been super busy at work."

"Bruh," Markell said. "We know you're busy. But how are you? No one's heard from you. And I know everyone's checked on you since the mass text about the breakup."

"It's not a breakup if we were never together," I said. I didn't know why I was saying it like that. Denial, I guess. "Dustin's in Chicago. I'm here. We're moving on."

"The lies we tell," Manessa said, clacking their fingernails in unison with each word. Tongue pop. Rolled their eyes. "You're always there for everyone else, girl. Let us be here for you."

Markell helped Manessa take out white cardboard cartons and black plastic containers. They'd picked up food from my favorite Chinese restaurant. I reached into the dishwasher and took out three clean plates and forks. We weren't going to eat with the plastic utensils that came with the takeout order.

"Thank you," I said as I set the plates and forks nearby on the island. "I feel bad for being out of touch. I feel bad the folks sent you on a rescue mission to find me."

"Everyone's been asking about you at Beaux," Markell said. "Everyone's like, 'Where's Taylor?'"

"That's flattering," I said. I appreciated their attempts to make me smile. Not that I'd had much of a reason to smile lately in my personal life. "I guess I just lost track of time and got wrapped up in work. It's busy. I'm so sorry."

"Girl," Manessa said. Tongue pop. "You ain't gotta apologize. We know how you going through it with work. We'll be at Miss Coco's graduation ceremony next week."

"Commencement is my favorite time of year," I said. I hoped my smile didn't come across as fake. I knew I was lying. Not about commencement season being fun. But that I was turning to work to hide how I was really feeling. "It's always so fun and celebratory."

Markell grabbed my shoulders and looked at me square in the face. "We've been besties and brothers for most of our lives. I know when you're faking it. That's why we're here."

Manessa scooped rice, green beans, beef and broccoli, egg rolls, and other items onto plates, and I broke down.

"All right," I said. "I'm not doing well at all. I miss Dustin. I said some stupid and insensitive things to him. The layers of his life kept unfolding in front of me—all truth, but all secretive nonetheless. We just decided to go our separate ways. I didn't want to come around because I was embarrassed and felt stupid and like a failure. And I don't fail. I never should have gotten involved with Dustin, but now that he's gone, I wish we'd worked things out. And I miss him. I miss him, and I like him, and I hate him all at the same time. I can't believe I'm saying this out loud. You are both what I needed."

Markell hugged me from the front. Manessa, who'd finished organizing our dinner plates, hugged me from behind.

"I don't even know what you like about my dumbass, big head cousin anyway," Manessa said. Tongue pop. Laugh. "What are you gonna do?"

We stayed in our hugging formation as I answered.

"Well, Dustin and I are done," I said. "I'm not doing

anything. I'm getting over him. I'm not chasing him. He's two thousand miles away and not moving back."

"And y'all have not talked?" Markell asked and pulled away. Manessa did the same. "You're not even going to try?"

"We both made choices," I said. "And we didn't choose us. So, nothing to try."

"You sure about that, Taylor?" Markell asked. "It would make me so happy to see you with someone. That's if being with someone is what you want."

"Dustin has made it clear he doesn't want to be with me," I said. "And I'm going to move on, even if it hurts for a little while. Besides, I'm getting my materials together for a campus president job that's going to be posted soon."

"Oh wow." Markell put his hands up to high-five me. "Congratulations. What campus?"

"Well, I don't have the job yet, and I don't want to jinx it. But that's another reason I've been off the grid lately, besides trying to get over Dustin. No time for any kind of relationship anyway, whether it's Dustin or anyone else."

I shrugged and put my hands up in front of me. I was sure I was disappointing Markell for my relationship stance. I was equally sure I was disappointing Manessa for not wanting to get back with Dustin, though we had never really been together.

"As long as you're sure," Markell said. He was starting to mix three tequila and tonic drinks for us. "I won't bother you about Dustin or relationships anymore."

"I'm more than sure," I said. "I'll be okay."

Manessa began moving our food plates to the living room.

"Well, that's a word," Manessa said. Tongue pop. "Then I say let's get to *Drag Race* before our food gets cold and it gets too late. I'm doing the late-night show at Beaux tonight. You should come out, even if it's a school night."

An hour later, when the show ended, Markell and Manessa got up and took their empty plates and glasses to the kitchen sink.

"One day, a bitch is gonna be on that show." Manessa snapped their fingers with the be-on-that-show phrase. "Until then, I'll be doing all my nights in the Castro."

"You run the show," I said. "Better not tell Miss Coco Hydrate I said that."

Manessa reached out to me and pulled me into a hug.

"I'm sorry things didn't work out for you and my dumbass cousin."

"It's fine," I said. "It was good while it lasted. You and I are still friends."

"Well, I can stay if you want to talk some more," Markell said, joining the group hug. "All I have is my husband to go home to, and he's grading finals, so I'll basically be going to an empty apartment tonight and for the next week or so until he's done for the semester. You'd think I'd be used to the academic life and schedule, with you, your parents, and Nate in it. Maybe I'll pick up an extra shift at Beaux just to pass the time."

"Thank you both for stopping by," I said. "Even though it was unannounced, it was what I needed. I promise I will reach out if I get in my feelings or get in a funk."

After Markell and Manessa left, I turned the TV off and put the leftover Chinese food in the refrigerator. Like I usually did on Sunday evenings before getting in bed and going to sleep, I opened my tablet. I needed to review my Monday meetings schedule and to see if anything had popped up in email I needed to handle. Nothing. Not even a Sunday evening curveball from Wes Jenkins. I typed "Dustin McMillan" in the email search for anything new from him about the accreditation process. Nothing new there in the main email or spam. Our work connection would end in a matter of days, and then our story would be history.

Markell and Manessa's spontaneous visit made me smile. It made me feel good they wanted to check in on me despite my disappearing act on them for the past weeks. Even though I still carried some sadness over how things turned out with Dustin, I felt ready to move forward. I had no choice.

CHAPTER SIXTEEN

Dustin

Every morning at sunrise since returning to Chicago nearly a month ago, I got up and ran along Lake Michigan before starting work. Every morning while running, I thought about Taylor.

Random thoughts. Random conversations. Random memories.

Seeing him for the first time at Beaux in San Francisco.

Teasing him about how much or how little he tipped the drag performers at the Beyoncé-themed *Renaissance* show.

Being rejected by him initially.

Learning we'd be working together on the Cal U Lake Merced accreditation process. How random was that? Grateful.

Being obnoxious, but all in line of doing my job, at Taylor's first accreditation presentation.

Driving to the Napa Valley retreat together.

Enjoying being outside at Crissy Field and the views of the Golden Gate Bridge.

Bonding over the smash-and-grab car break-in experience.

Being assigned as roommates at the retreat and learning more about how great Taylor was…I mean is.

Sleeping in the same bed at the retreat, being so close to touch, and touching but not doing anything.

Growing in our respect for each other's professional skills and presence at the retreat.

Appreciating and bonding over our mutual dislike of Wes Jenkins.

Taking Taylor to meet my mom and eating the delicious homemade meal she made for us.

Kissing Taylor for the first time the night of dinner at my mom's place.

Opening up and being vulnerable about our lives, loves, and likes.

I let the memories and flashbacks of Taylor and me stop there. I didn't want to go negative. Only wanted to remember the good times. The hold he had on me. I couldn't explain. Yet I knew. I knew I loved him. I knew I should stop. Taylor was just so lovable. I couldn't get him out of my head. I'd probably love him for eternity.

On several occasions, my cousin Manessa would call or videochat to goad me into going back to San Francisco and fixing things with Taylor. Most days, I'd turn off my phone notifications because I didn't want to hear the same thing, almost daily, from Manessa.

Pride and ego.

I knew I should make some effort. I knew I made a stupid choice letting a few words get in the way of Taylor and me. I knew it was hasty to leave the Bay Area, knowing I could have finished the job assignment there and also knowing I was in the middle of rebuilding relationships with my mom and the rest of my family. A lot had changed in the time Taylor had come into my life. He'd made quite an impact on me, much like he'd done for others in his professional, civic, and personal life.

Pride and ego. I wasn't going to be the one to reach out. Even though I really wanted to.

❖

That morning was different, however. Something wouldn't let me sleep. I was hot. I tossed and turned in bed most of the night. I couldn't get Taylor out of my head. Tired of the random thoughts of Taylor that filled my mind, I got up a little after three in the morning, made a cup of coffee, and went to my laptop and desk to work. I churned out the final accreditation letter for California University Lake Merced in about an hour. I'd hoped that finishing the project once and for all would give me the closure I needed to get over Taylor and anything related to the Bay Area.

After finishing my morning run and making it back to my apartment, I checked my email to make sure the final copy of the report recommending reaccreditation for Cal U Lake Merced had made it to President Weatherspoon, Taylor, their respective assistants including Wes Jenkins, and to my supervisors at the Kane-Carlos Collective. I was glad I made the choice to finish the project.

The email had gone through successfully to all recipients. This would be my last correspondence with Taylor. I hoped it would make him happy and give him what he needed for his career aspirations. He was definitely going places. I wished I was going with him. But that chapter, like my work with California University Lake Merced, was closed.

Now, with the assignment over, I planned to take a two-week break, which the Kane-Carlos Collective built into the process after finishing one project and before getting assigned to a new one. The break would be perfect for me. I needed to get to know Chicago again. And with the weather in late spring and early summer being as close to perfect as it could be here, I planned to hit some neighborhood food festivals, explore the North Halsted strip they used to call Boystown, and maybe get into a friend group again. Do some things and get a life to take my mind off Taylor. My heart was broken, but I needed to move on and live.

I picked up my phone and turned off the Do Not Disturb feature. Dozens of missed texts and calls from Manessa this morning. Wasn't going to call back. Who needed another lecture from Manessa about Taylor and me? After taking a long and hot shower soon, I was going to keep all notifications off and enjoy my solo and quiet time. At least for a day.

Manessa was relentless, however, and was now video calling me. I picked up this time.

"Damn, Manessa, you been blowing up my phone all morning," I said. "What's up?"

"You need to get back to the Bay Area right now. It's your ma."

CHAPTER SEVENTEEN

Taylor

Two weeks after Dustin's mother's funeral, I sat with him in the kitchen where I'd met and had dinner with his mom for the first and only time all those weeks ago in Oakland. That was the first time Dustin and I hung out together outside of our work project. The first time I had an inkling we might have a connection beyond platonic friendship or professional kinship.

"What do you need from me?" I asked as we sat on barstools at the kitchen island counter. "How can I help?"

"Thank you for being here," Dustin said. He sipped on a short glass of Hennessy on ice, moving a small box of leftover obituaries to the side of the counter to make room for a few containers of burgers, fries, and sodas I had picked up on the way to Oakland. "Thanks for bringing something to eat other than catering from Lena's Soul Food."

We laughed. No words needed. Black families and funerals. Soul food delivered daily like clockwork for about two weeks.

"I figured you could use a change of pace," I said. "I also figured you probably hadn't had dinner yet."

"I had a smoothie earlier and lost track of time." He unwrapped one of the two identical burger combination plates, taking a bite and swallowing before he continued. "You're too kind. I know you've been juggling graduation and now summer orientation season duties while being here for me and for my mom's service. You ain't have to do all that for me."

"I know I didn't have to. I wanted to."

And I did. No questions asked.

When Manessa told me Dustin was coming back to the Bay Area to handle his mother's business, I knew there was no other place I'd be than by Dustin's side. I didn't need to, but I picked him up at the Oakland International Airport when he arrived from Chicago. I also arranged a car rental to be delivered to his mom's house because I figured he'd need to run errands, and a rental was cheaper than calling rideshares. I pretty much stayed by his side when I wasn't on the San Francisco side at the Cal U Lake Merced summer orientation activities and attending meet-and-greets with supporters of prospective students.

In between, with President Weatherspoon's knowledge and blessing, I'd started the interview and background vetting process for a few campus presidency jobs I'd thrown my hat into the ring for. It had been a lot for my schedule, but Dustin needed someone by his side to run ideas, to get another perspective, and to help make decisions his brother Dorian would have helped with had he been able to get more than a forty-eight-hour furlough for the funeral services.

No words were needed or exchanged about the last time we'd seen each other, the night of the quiet argument between us in the Hotel Castro, when Dustin decided to leave for Chicago. No words about the month apart. No words about what I felt, at least, when he was away. No words about when he was going back. It wasn't the time or place. All that mattered to me was helping Dustin in his time of bereavement.

"I appreciate you," Dustin said. "I really do."

"No problem."

"As you can see, everyone has come and gone," he said. "Someone once told me, and now I know it's true, that the loneliest time when losing a parent ain't the actual moment you learn they're gone. It's when the people stop visiting or calling and the fried chicken stops arriving."

Dustin and I smiled at his attempt at humor. The night before, we'd cleaned the leftover chicken, salads, green beans, and macaroni and cheese that Dustin's family and his mom's friends had delivered out of the refrigerator. Once the guest visits dwindled, including a surprise visit from Dustin's dad, and it was down to Dustin, Manessa, and me primarily, there was no need to keep so much old food around.

"I'll be here as long as you need me."

"Thanks," Dustin said. "I have a lot of shit to figure out. I might take you up on your offer."

"You just tell me what you need."

"First, a hug?" Dustin asked. He got up from his barstool by the counter and walked toward me. "Just a hug. I'm not trying to do anything else now."

I reached out my arms toward him. "I trust you. I wouldn't try anything else more than a hug right now."

We pulled each other into an embrace and stood still for what seemed like minutes, his sandalwood and my cocoa butter aromas floating around us, our breathing in sync with each other.

"I'm glad you're here, Doc," he said, still embracing me, the humming of his voice and heartbeat against mine. The sound of Dustin calling me Doc was familiar and nice. It made me think of the good times we'd had getting to know each other and more. "I couldn't have done this without you. You're the only one I trusted to be there for me."

"I wouldn't be anywhere else. I'm glad I could be here for you."

We pulled apart and sat back down on our respective stools by the counter. Dustin took another sip of his drink. I sipped on a bottled water.

"I also want to thank you, Doc."

"I think you've done that enough. I'm gonna get embarrassed."

"Just let me say this," he said. "If I hadn't met you, I probably wouldn't have reached out to my ma. I probably wouldn't have grown in my patience and attempts to understand her. I probably wouldn't have had time with her at all. And now, I might get to know my dad after all these years. I am going to get to know him. Even though I don't know how to know someone after forty years. But here I am. Thanks, Doc."

"That was *all* you," I said. "You made the choice. You're making it. All you."

Dustin started laughing.

"I couldn't believe all the surprisingly kind things people said about my ma," he said. "It was nice and funny hearing all these people talk about how she was there for them. And I was sitting there the whole time trying to figure out how she had the time or means to be so generous. I mean all the neighborhood kids she packed lunches for and the after-school dinners she made for them when they came home alone from school while waiting for their parents to come home from work. Sewing dresses and costumes for Manessa, Coco Hydrate, and their performer friends. Riding the buses out to the casinos with the elderly elders and giving them some pocket change that I probably gave to her, so that they could play a few rounds of slots. I was in awe just listening to how generous she was."

"I heard it all, too."

"It brings tears to my eyes now thinking about how they see...saw...things in my ma that I didn't see," Dustin said. "Granted, I probably financed most of her generosity. But this whole time I thought she and the rest of the family were just using me for themselves. I hate that I spent so much time away, being embarrassed and avoiding my family and my upbringing."

"True," I said. "But on the positive side, you got a few weeks with her when you came back for the Lake Merced job. You got to have some sense of reconciliation. Or at least some sense of relationship again with her."

Dustin smiled at me, eyes overflowing with tears that were gliding down his face. I handed him a napkin.

"That is what you've done for me," Dustin said. "And I'll be eternally grateful for your role in that relationship piece with my ma. And now, hopefully, my dad. I couldn't believe how he showed up to her services and came by the house. Dorian's father, too. You did this, Saint Taylor."

"Stop, Dustin," I said. "I'm the one who should be saying kind and comforting words to you. After what you've been and are going through."

"You know I tend to pour it on thick," Dustin said. He laughed and dabbled his face and eyes to dry the tears. "I know at times I can be obnoxious, cocky, and overly confident trying to be someone's number one. I wanna tell you all the things that I appreciate about you. Can I at least do that?"

"Can I give it back? Some compliments and comfort?"

"You can try, Doc. You might not compare."

We laughed and stood up again from our barstools.

"Well, at least let me apologize," I said. "That night. That comment."

I'd felt guilty for weeks implying Dustin was a distraction to my career goals. He wasn't. In fact, if anything, I knew that he knew about my work, what it took to be successful and advance in the field, and more importantly, me.

He pulled me into another embrace. "Doc, you ain't gotta

apologize for being you. You're a career person. Isn't that what we all—well, most of us—want in a long-term partner anyway? We ain't gotta revisit that night. Though I probably owe you more apologies than you owe me."

"Fine," I said. "Let's just call it a draw. No apologies needed. Are you going to let me go or just keep hugging me like this?"

He kissed my cheek and released the hug. We remained holding hands, though.

"I missed you."

"I missed you."

"I was so fucking stubborn," he said. "If this hadn't happened with my ma, I wonder who would have reached out first? Would we have found each other again?"

"Doesn't matter," I said. "All that matters is here and now. And me being here for you for as long as you need."

"Well, I love you, Doc. I want you here for as long as you want to be."

Wait, had Dustin just said the word "love"? Why had he said this now? The deliriousness and confusion of grief? The heat of the moment, without any heat?

"Are you sure you meant to say what you said?" I asked. "There's no pressure or anything from me if you…"

"I said what I said, Doc. Just take it. You don't have to say it back, not that I want you to leave me hanging like that night when I first told you I liked you. I'm just saying how I feel. Trust, it's not grief. It's not me being needy because of my ma. Just receive it. No reciprocation needed."

I slid my hands out of his and raised one to Dustin's face and beard. He smiled at me again, and I smiled back. In that moment I knew what I felt for Dustin. I knew what I'd felt all along, even during the weeks that he'd gone back to Chicago after our quiet argument. I loved him, too. I couldn't believe I was waking up and feeling a feeling. A feeling I couldn't deny any longer.

"What if I want to reciprocate?"

"What are you saying, Doc?"

I looked into his eyes, smiled, and traced my fingers along his mouth. This wasn't the appropriate time for anything beyond fingers on face, so I put my hands in his hands again.

"I love you, Dustin."

"Are you sure?" Dustin asked. "You're not just saying it because I said it?"

"I am *so* sure. I am one hundred percent sure."

We tilted our foreheads forward and let them rest against the other. It felt intimate. It felt warm. It felt right. It was enough. That was all Dustin and I needed at that moment.

CHAPTER EIGHTEEN

Dustin

"I've always wanted to come here," Taylor said to me as we pulled up in the rental car to the valet station outside the restaurant. "What a nice surprise to end the week."

We needed a change of pace from focusing on me and my loss, even if for just one early Friday summer evening. I made us a dinner reservation at the Lake Chalet restaurant, set on Lake Merritt in the center of Oakland. The temperature outside was just right—not too warm, and the evening chill hadn't set in yet—and the sky clear so we could enjoy another scenic location we would add to our roster of nature spots we'd enjoyed together.

If the evening went as I'd planned, it would make not only Taylor's week, but his life. I couldn't wait for the evening to unfold. My nerves were out of control trying to keep it together.

"Before we go in, let's do some selfies as the kids would do," I said. I was stalling just to make sure everything went as planned. I handed the valet service person my keys and a twenty-dollar bill tip to look after the car and leave it within eyesight. "Do you mind, Doc? We won't miss our reservation."

We walked from the valet and street side of the restaurant on the path that led us around to the Lake Merritt side. We oohed and aahed at the views of the water, the skyline in the distance, and the apartment buildings and hills on the other side of the lake. It was a warm evening but not unbearable. Taylor looked amazing in his light blue seersucker suit, which coordinated well with my tan seersucker suit. I extended my arm and phone to get pics of Taylor and me in multiple poses, with various waterfront scenes behind us.

"Are you two a couple?" I heard a voice near Taylor and me call to us. It made me flash back to that time we were at Crissy Field near the Golden Gate Bridge, the first time someone asked if Taylor and I were together. Back then, without hesitation, we had both had said no because, at the time, we weren't a couple, just colleagues on a work project. "We can take your photo if you want, if you take one of us."

"We'd love it," Taylor said without hesitation. "We are."

It surprised me to hear those words from Taylor since Taylor and I hadn't discussed our status since my return to the Bay Area.

"We are," I said in a matter-of-fact but questioning way. "We are."

"Well, you two look amazing," one of the couple said to Taylor and me after taking dozens of pictures of us. They handed back my phone and handed me one of theirs to take pictures of them. "What's the occasion?"

Taylor and I looked at each other and smiled.

"Just dinner," I said quickly. "Just an end-of-the-week TGIF dinner."

"Same for us," the other of the couple said to us. "If there's ever an occasion, a party, or a gathering, we'd love to connect. We just moved out here from Chicago about a month ago and are looking for other Black gay couples and a friend group."

"What a coincidence," I said. "I just moved back here from Chicago after a couple years."

"You've moved," Taylor said in a matter-of-fact but

questioning way to me. Then he pivoted back to the couple. "We'd love to connect. I'm Taylor. This is Dustin."

After a few minutes of exchanging small talk and social media information with each other, the couple—Logan and Jordan—walked toward the restaurant while I opened up the photos on my phone for us to look at.

"We do look good," I said as I swiped. "We're a couple?"

"I agree, we do look good," Taylor said as he looked at the pictures, our cheeks touching. "You're back here in the Bay Area? Oakland?"

At the same time, we said yes and smiled at each other. We were present in the moment. I was glad to be there and happy to do something special for Taylor, especially after all he'd done for me.

I'd decided to stay in the Bay Area for a few more weeks to take care of the business that comes with losing a parent, for which there is no manual. I was in total gratitude for Taylor, who hadn't yet experienced the same loss himself, but who had stayed by my side and helped me the entire time while doing his full-time work at the university. All I thought was about how much I loved that man for being present and for just being.

"We've been waiting for you, Drs. James and McMillan," the host said when I shared our reservation information. "We'll get you seated in just a moment."

I saw our photo-op friends, Logan and Jordan, sitting and waiting nearby. They explained their reservation got pushed back for being a few minutes late, probably due to our pictures and socializing on the lakefront side of the restaurant.

"Can they join our reservation?" Taylor asked the host and me. "It'll give us a chance to talk more and welcome them to the Bay Area."

The host confirmed there was room for our new

acquaintances, and they led us through the restaurant bar area, which had filled up with the post-work happy hour professional crowd.

"Your table and seats are a little bit off this area here," the host said, smiling and winking at me. I was nervous they'd give the evening's agenda away.

We arrived at the private dining room area I'd reserved. As planned, all the guests I'd invited had arrived on time and were in place to shout "surprise" to Taylor when we entered the room—Taylor's parents from L.A., Markell and Nate, Manessa and Coco Hydrate, President Weatherspoon and her partner, Taylor's mentee and student assistant Justin Monroe— all the people who were important to Taylor and now to me in some way. Even my dad showed up, an invitation I'd never expected him to respond to. Plus Logan and Jordan, who had no idea what they were doing here except for a spontaneous dinner invitation, but joined in the surprise and festive moment anyway.

Taylor looked stunned. His mouth opened wide, and he cupped his hand over his face. His eyes started to tear up.

"Is this what I think it is?" Taylor asked me as he looked around the room filled with our important people. "Mom. Dad. Oh, my goodness. I am not prepared for this."

"It is and it isn't," I said, grabbing one of Taylor's hands. "We will be engaged one day, I'm sure of it, if that's what we want. But that's not what this evening is about."

Taylor fanned his face and eyes. I was happy the surprise dinner had gone off without a hitch. Everyone was on time, except Wes Jenkins, who hadn't yet arrived.

"So, what is it about?" Taylor asked. "I don't know if I can take any more surprises."

A member of the waitstaff carried around flutes of champagne to the dinner party. I walked Taylor to his seat at the head of the table, and I nodded to President Weatherspoon, who looked regal with a colorful and flowy Afrocentric caftan and an updo of halo braids that reminded me of Texas Congresswoman Sheila Jackson Lee, to begin comments.

"Dr. James, you're brilliant," President Weatherspoon said as she raised a glass to Taylor and to the guests. "You championed the accreditation process for California University Lake Merced, with many internal and external challenges. In spite of them, we got reaccredited for eight years. That is a positive for our campus and for you. On behalf of the Lake Merced campus community, thank you. Let's toast to Taylor."

Wes Jenkins entered and appeared surprised to be in a room of guests. I motioned for him to take an empty seat at the table as I walked to the front of the room where the audiovisual equipment was.

"So, I'm really excited for this next speaker," I said. "California University Chancellor Christine Hosoda couldn't join us in Oakland today, but she is joining us live via Zoom from Long Beach. She has some special words for Taylor and for others here at Lake Chalet today. Let me see if I can get her linked in now."

I wasn't the best with technology but managed to get Chancellor Hosoda up on screen.

"Good evening, Dr. Taylor James, friends, and colleagues," Chancellor Hosoda said, with the California University system backdrop and logo behind her. "I'm so pleased to be with you all today. As President Weatherspoon shared, Dr. James, or Taylor, as everyone gathered at your celebration dinner calls you, we're so proud of you and the job you did with the accreditation process at Cal U Lake Merced. Thank you."

I looked around the room and could see Taylor's eyes lit up, and his parents' faces beaming with pride.

"Dr. James, let me get to the point so you all can get

on with your festivities in Oakland," Chancellor Hosoda continued. "You've been a trusted and valued member of President Weatherspoon's cabinet and leadership team, and a respected leader within the California University system for years. You did this on your own, even though you could have ridden on the coattails of your parents, renowned scholars and leaders themselves within the Cal U system. Because of this, I am pleased to announce that at the next Board of Trustees meeting later this summer, you will be named to lead your own cabinet at the California University Oakland campus. Congratulations, soon-to-be President Taylor James."

My eyes watered. Taylor's eyes watered. Taylor's parents ran to him and hugged him. The rest of the guests, except for Wes Jenkins, rose and applauded Taylor. We all were proud of Taylor's dream coming true. I walked over to Taylor and gave him a kiss before ending with one final piece of the program before dinner.

"Did you want to add anything, President Weatherspoon or Chancellor Hosoda?" I asked.

"Let's just leave it at this for now," President Weatherspoon said. "This evening is about celebrating Taylor. The rest I'll deal with and make announcements on campus next week."

Based on a conversation President Weatherspoon arranged with me about the accreditation process and my thoughts on the Cal U Lake Merced team working with Taylor, I had an idea, but wasn't completely sure what her announcement would be. It was enough, though, to see Wes Jenkins's face as he heard about Taylor's next career move. Anytime that I could do petty on Taylor's behalf, especially when it came to Wes Jenkins, I was game.

As I worked to disconnect the audiovisual equipment, the Lake Chalet staff set up the buffet of starters, salads, and seafood specialties for our dinner. D.J. Kidd, one of Taylor's former students at the Lake Merced campus and now a successful party promoter in L.A., the Bay Area, and other large markets starved of Black & queer scenes, kicked off the music with some old-school jams for the elders. Later, we'd advance to more current day music for a night of dancing. Taylor clinked his glass and stood up. He motioned for Kidd to pause the music.

"I have a few words to offer before we eat. I am thrilled, honored, and surprised to see my favorite people and loved ones, even you, Wes Jenkins, here to celebrate me today. But everything I am is because of you. And so, I'd like to toast each one of you."

Taylor pulled out a piece of paper from his suit jacket pocket as he spoke. It made me wonder, had he known about this surprise dinner in his honor?

"Wes Jenkins—you keep me on my toes, that's for sure. President Weatherspoon—your leadership has inspired me for years, both as a family friend and also as my supervisor. I will take many lessons from you with me as I start my presidency at Cal U Oakland. Manessa and Coco Hydrate—I've watched you grow and develop as performers and as scholars at Cal U Lake Merced. I'm proud of you both finishing your degrees and will have your back with whatever your next steps are in your drag life, your personal life, and your professional life. Little Justin, my mentee, and now J.J. Monroe—I'm so happy to have seen you mature from a college first-year student to graduating soon. I can't wait to see you follow in your father's footsteps in television news. Markell, my brother bestie, and Nate, my brother who loves my brother—you have been a lifeline to me since I moved to the Bay Area five years ago. I love you more than you know. My mom and dad—words cannot express how much I have felt your unconditional love and support since I can remember. I appreciate you pushing me to be better, do better, and to always strive for excellence. I am such a lucky son. I hope one day that I, too, can have an almost fifty-year marriage."

Taylor walked over to me with a huge smile on his face. I smiled back and wondered what he'd have to say to, for, and about me.

"And Dr. McMillan...Dustin, D.J., Junior, the obnoxious stranger I met at Beaux in the Castro all those months ago at a Sunday Funday drag brunch. I hated you, then strongly disliked you, then respected you, then liked you, then had to pretend I didn't like you, then ultimately loved you. I never thought I'd make time or meet someone like you who would love me, my quirks, flaws, and all. Thank you. I love you."

"I love you, too, Taylor. I am so proud of you."

"Let me finish," Taylor said. "I have since learned what you were carrying about yourself and your life before we met. I grew to appreciate how you opened up to me about you. I appreciate how, ultimately, you came around to embrace your cousin Manessa and your mom. Even your dad, now. Family means a lot to me—there's nothing more important. I know it's becoming important to you, especially since your mom passed recently. I want to be your family. I want to embrace your family. I knew something was up for today, but I didn't know what exactly."

"Doc, you knew?" I hugged him and then said to our guests, "This man is too smart. I can't get anything past him."

Taylor motioned to our new acquaintances, Logan and Jordan, who stood up and walked our way. Now I was wondering what was in store for the evening.

"There are no coincidences," Taylor said. He started tearing up again, which made me tear up. "Logan is a former student of mine who is now an attorney who volunteers with an organization that helps those who can't afford strong legal representation appeal their cases, especially if they were unjustly convicted. I contacted him shortly after I met your dear, sweet mother. He found new evidence and a loophole in your brother Dorian's case, and thanks to Logan's work, Dorian will be coming home in a few weeks. I only wish this could have happened before—"

What a saint.

My love for Taylor exploded. My heart. I started ugly crying on Taylor's shoulder in front of our guests.

"I love you, Doc," I said in between huffs and dry heaving. "This evening was supposed to be about you."

Taylor laughed and pointed to his mom.

"Many of you know my mom can't hold water," he said while smiling in her direction. "When she asked me about the menu at Lake Chalet and what's there to do around Lake Merritt in Oakland, I had a feeling something was up. And then when my phone started pinging yesterday and today with her location near the Bay Area, because she forgot to turn off the Share My Location feature, I definitely knew something was going on."

The audience laughed as Taylor's dad brought me a clean linen napkin to dry my eyes. I, the obnoxious one with no feeling, no emotion, was suddenly full of feeling and emotions. Again, all I could think was how much I loved Taylor.

"I love your son so much, Dr. and Dr. James," I said. I didn't know what else to say. I felt like a blubbering mess in front of Taylor's important people. The petty in me loved that Wes Jenkins was seeing and hearing all this love and celebration for Taylor. "I am beside myself. I am surprised. Thank you, Taylor, for getting my brother back to me…my family."

Taylor hugged me and held my free hand that didn't have the wet linen napkin in it.

"Can you handle one more, Dustin?" Taylor asked me.

My brother's coming back to me. Taylor's promotion to a campus president. Both were enough for me. "What else is there?"

"Jordan here," Taylor said, "is another former student of mine. He and Logan are a couple and they live here in the Bay Area."

"Wait, no Chicago?" I asked and looked at Jordan, then Logan, then Taylor. "What's going on? The whole 'are you two a couple' thing on the waterfront? What was that all about?"

"Jordan is a wedding planner," Taylor said. "I had a feeling something was happening today, but I didn't know what. So, I asked Jordan and Logan to stage the phone pictures, and Jordan, the wedding planner, had other photographers and drones stationed to take our pre-engagement, and now engagement photos."

"Wait, what the heck?" Now my mouth was wide open. I could hear gasps and cheers coming from our guests. "What's going on?"

Jordan handed a small box to Taylor. Logan handed a small box to me.

"Dustin," Taylor said, opening the box in his hand. In it, I saw a simple yet beautiful black ring. "We're not getting married today or anytime soon. But I'd like...*love*...for you to be my person. My forever person. Will you?"

I was completely shocked and surprised. I knew what my answer would be. But then I remembered how Taylor delayed responding to me both times I self-disclosed any feelings for liking him or loving him.

"Y'all," I said. I kept a smile on my face as I moved around and did a Manessa tongue pop and flicked my nonexistent and imaginary long weave. "Let me break the scene and use a little gay vernacular for a bit. This bitch...this bitch left me on read not once, but twice. First when I told him I liked him. He made me wait in silence. And then when I told him I loved him. He made me wait one more time in silence. So, let's pull a Beyoncé and all get on mute while I decide if I'ma be Taylor's forever person."

I put my hand in the air to signal quiet and no movement, much like Beyoncé did during the song "Energy" at her Renaissance World tour. I stared around the room and saw everyone freeze for about thirty seconds before I put my hand and ring finger out in front of Taylor.

"Of course I'ma be your forever person."

"And I'm going to be *your* forever person."

After we put our respective rings on each other's fingers, our guests clapped and cheered. I pulled Taylor toward me, first into a hug, and then sealed the deal of forever with a kiss.

CHAPTER NINETEEN

Taylor

"Cheers to Dorian and new beginnings! Cheers to Markell's promotion to general manager! Cheers to Taylor and Dustin!"

We tapped our shot glasses on the counter, and I downed what would be my first and only tequila shot of the evening.

We were celebrating a lot. Dorian's recent release from Solano. Markell's new title at the bar, since some of his colleagues were striking out on a new nightclub venture they were calling the Pink Swallow a few blocks away in the Castro neighborhood. Dustin's and my engagement. And of course, my upcoming role as a campus president.

I'd taken my first significant time off from work since resigning from and transitioning out of California University Lake Merced. Soon after my two weeks off, my transition meetings with the California University Oakland team would begin, which would prepare me for my official start as campus president at the beginning of fall semester. Two weeks of free time during summer in the Bay Area excited me.

I had a lot to do. I had to find a new place in the East Bay. I had to pack up my current place. I had tons of paperwork to fill out with the Oakland campus and with the chancellor's office. Dustin and I had preliminary meetings with Jordan to discuss ceremony and reception ideas, though we were long away from setting any dates. For most people, time off was a time to relax, and to sleep in for a few days. But for me, it was time to prep for my next chapter. And to get a little sleep.

This early evening, however, was not about work. It was a different sort of education and test. And it would be more than a one-and-done kind of evening.

Dustin and I sat at Markell's bar well at Beaux on my first Monday of freedom, the same seats where we first met. Now, as a couple and as a found family, we were sampling drinks mixed by Dorian, Dustin's brother, whom Markell had hired to work as a barback and fill-in bartender during Markell's weekday happy hour shifts.

I looked at the drink flight board that Dorian sat in front of me. On it were samplers of the more popular drinks bought at the bar—a Cadillac margarita, a sidecar, a Cape Cod, a vodka tonic, and a negroni. Thankfully, we were catching a rideshare to my place near Lake Merced after Dorian's cocktail school.

"I think you've passed, Dorian," I said after taking a sip of each drink. They were really good and mixed to perfection. "You're a quick study. You're going to give Markell a run for his money here."

"Bet," Dorian said, giving Markell a high five. "Thanks for the opportunity, my new brotha. I ain't gonna let you down."

"Oh, I know you won't," Markell said. "We're too interconnected now. Your brother and my bestie-brother being together. You working here with me. There's no room for any of us to fuck up."

"Most definitely," Dustin said. "I'm proud of you, Dorian. Thank you, Markell, for hiring my brother. Thank you, Taylor, for just about everything."

"Amen," Dorian said. "To that, Markell, can we do another shot? I've kept track of how many promos and comps

I've used. Plus, I can't wait to tell you about all the ideas I have for the bar."

"We can do another round if you can pass the test," Markell said. "What are the three personalities of Beaux, but pretty much any bar here in Castro?"

Dorian smiled, showing off his quick study skills, and answered, "You got the happy hour crowd that skews older, then the clubland night crowd kids, and then the drag brunch crowd of all ages, genders, races, and sexualities. I'm as smart as the docs over here."

I smiled and rolled my eyes. I always felt weird when people heaped compliments and gratitude on me. I knew it was something, a big deal, especially to them. But at the same time, it wasn't a big deal to me. To me, it was just doing the right thing to help out, to use my life for good, to leverage my privilege to uplift others.

"I know you ain't fixing to do no shots without us," Manessa said as they entered the bar with Coco Hydrate, Justin Monroe, who now went by J.J. Monroe, and the Beaux dancer who J.J. was now dating seriously. Signature tongue pop, eye roll, nail clacks, and hair flip punctuated the entrance. "But Coco and I will take these leftover flights instead. What y'all talking about? What's the deal today?"

While Dustin, Markell, and Dorian filled in Manessa, Coco, and J.J. about the goings-on at Monday happy hour, I drifted off in thought like I usually did.

For the first time in a long time, I felt happy, truly happy.

I looked at this little group I was a part of, this group of Black and queer and fluid people who found each other in San Francisco, a city where there weren't a lot of us. Everyone liked to attribute bringing us together to me, but in reality, it was because of what Markell built for us here during his happy hour shifts at Beaux. He made a safe space where we could be proudly Black, openly queer, and curiously open about ourselves and our likes, dislikes, wants, and desires. This was a space in San Francisco, a community space in a Castro bar, of all places, that every Black, queer person wanted and deserved, especially in a city where it was hard to find each other. They may have wanted to toast and cheer me for what they say I'd done for them, but they'd given more to me than I ever could have done for them. More than they would ever know.

I worked out in my mind what our next steps would be in terms of living arrangements. I'd let Dorian have my apartment near Lake Merced so he wouldn't have to commute so far to his new job at Beaux. We'd get Silas out of Dustin's place in Dogpatch and let Manessa and Coco Hydrate have it, so they wouldn't have to commute so far for their performances in San Francisco. I'd move in with Dustin at the Oakland house he'd renovated for his mom, so that my commute to California University Oakland would be easy. Of course, we'd move out all her furniture, or at least give first dibs to Dorian, Manessa, and Coco, and bring in our own.

I looked at Dustin, who confidently commanded the space and conversation. His confidence, which I misread and disliked as arrogance in the beginning, was so attractive to me. I loved how he took charge with decisions for us. I loved how he could read the room after one of my busy days and give me space and quiet. I loved him.

I couldn't believe how much had changed in me, and for me, within the span of less than a year. Months.

Dustin.

So much for work and career being the only love of my life. So much for the belief that looks, life, and love were over after thirty in the queer community. The saying about how when you least expected and looked for love, it'd find you is true. Even if you blocked it, denied it, ignored it, pushed it away, fought it, it'd find you. It would take over. It certainly did me.

And I got a campus presidency. And I got Dustin.

I smiled in my head, in my daydream, and then, apparently, in real life.

Markell had started the daily streaming of Beyoncé's *Renaissance* project, which we still loved even after her other projects had been released, and the introduction to "I'm That Girl" jolted me out of my daydreaming.

"Penny for your thoughts," Dustin said as he stood behind me and wrapped his arms around me. "What are you thinking about?"

I kissed him on the cheek, smiled, and said, "You. Me. Us. And our happily ever after."

EPILOGUE

Taylor & Dustin

Six months later

"Doc, please don't let that newspaper article ruin this special day," Dustin said as he fastened the final button of Taylor's academic regalia around his neck. "You have earned this."

As Taylor and Dustin prepared to leave Taylor's new presidential suite for the start of the ceremony, Taylor took another look at the campus paper, which his new chief of staff delivered daily to his desk. Taylor and Dustin both paid little to no mind to the official campus photographers around them whose job was to capture the large, small, and candid details of the day. That was part of their new life—being in the spotlight, but pretending to be oblivious to it.

The campus newspaper at California University Oakland had run two dueling headlines above the masthead about its new leader, President Taylor James, the eighth president of the campus, who'd been on the job for a few months.

One headline highlighted the Presidential Investiture Ceremony, an academic event typically held within a new president's first year, which would start in just a few minutes. The formal ceremony signified the beginning of a campus's new chapter of university leadership. It also gave the university community, community guests, and other campus presidents an opportunity to witness the formal installation of the new leader. The story highlighted Taylor's meteoric career trajectory, his place in history as a young, Black, and openly gay president, and his engagement to Dustin.

The other headline, next to the celebratory headline about the investiture, highlighted the public salary and benefits Taylor received as the new campus president of California University Oakland. The story, and the campus community members interviewed for it, focused solely on numbers: $495,500 yearly salary, $75,000 yearly housing allowance, $15,000 yearly auto allowance, plus an appointment to full professor with tenure in the College of Education, should Taylor resign or be asked to resign from the president role.

What the stories didn't focus on, but Taylor would be happy to elucidate with the student reporter and certainly would during his speech, were the long hours and major issues a campus president was responsible for. California University Oakland had quite a few issues: building the trust of the campus with Title IX and harassment cases following former President Eubanks's resignation, the threat of a strike by all the unions representing faculty and staff, declining enrollment numbers, rising costs to keep the university operating, shared governance and campus consultation among competing interests, and developing more campus housing around and adjacent to the campus, which many forewarned as gentrification.

Taylor was the final decider and signatory on every aspect of the university, and ultimately was responsible for the well-being of the institution, almost two thousand faculty, three thousand staff, and twenty thousand students, their supporters, and alumni. Campus presidents worked hard, decided much, attended events nightly, and served in their job 24/7. Often, the work of the president went unthanked, underappreciated, and overly critiqued by those who didn't understand or aspire to such a leadership position.

"What have I signed up for?" Taylor said. "Look at what they did with our sister at Harvard. Can I handle this? Yes, I know what I signed up for. I prayed and prepared for this most of my life and career. I can handle this."

"You got what you wanted, that's for sure," Dustin said. "The job and the man. And you can handle this. You of all people."

"I'm so lucky. Thanks for being by my side and for being my sounding board."

Dustin kissed him. "I got you, Doc. We're in this together. Forever."

Taylor and Dustin glanced at the computer monitor on Taylor's desk, which was livestreaming the event, to look at the audience awaiting the start of the investiture. It was a sunny and surprisingly warm January day in Oakland for the outdoor event in the campus plaza. They could see Taylor's parents in the front row and other members of Taylor's family from L.A., along with Markell, Nate, Dorian, Manessa, Coco Hydrate, J.J., and many of the bartenders from Beaux and other Castro establishments nearby. They also could see President Weatherspoon and the other California University campus presidents sitting onstage in their academic regalia, along with CU Chancellor Christine Hosoda. The pomp and circumstance of it all.

Taylor looked at the campus newspaper one more time, but this time focused on a smaller headline and story at the bottom of the paper that focused on the arrest and termination of a California University employee from the Lake Merced campus.

"Wes Jenkins *would* make headlines on my special day." Taylor handed the paper to Dustin and laughed. "Contracting performers for events and paying an entertainment LLC he owned using campus funds. Basically, paying himself. Thank goodness J.J.'s smarts and journalism skills raised his suspicions about the attention Wes Jenkins was paying to student organization events, especially the BlaQueer Club, which was way below Wes's duties and responsibilities."

"Messy."

"Wes Jenkins wanted my vice president job so bad," Taylor said. "Now he's out of a job and may be facing time. It would be ironic if he ended up in Solano County."

"The irony."

"I wonder what tipped off President Weatherspoon's suspicions besides J.J.'s articles about student organization funding at Lake Merced?"

"I'm not saying it's me, but after my work with campus, President Weatherspoon *did* ask me what I thought of you, Wes Jenkins, and specifically his work during the accreditation process," Dustin said. "I mentioned how he'd done a few shady things with the initial accreditation report, our calendar appointments, and how he'd been trying to throw you under the bus during most of the process. Oh, and the unpaid invoices to Kane-Carlos Collective for the work we did that Wes Jenkins was supposed to take care of."

"I'm confused. But I'll let it go."

"Don't worry about it now, Doc." Dustin put the newspaper back on Taylor's desk. "In my work, it's always the one throwing daggers at others who got the most to hide and to lose. So, I told President Weatherspoon what I thought about Wes Jenkins, and she must have taken it from there. I've learned a lesson or two about keeping secrets and withholding information. Never again with you or anyone else."

"I trust you," Taylor said. "My mom used to always say something to me and Markell like 'ask for protection from people who are being strategic with us while we are being genuine with them.' I guess there's truth to that. It's not going to stop me from being nice and generous. It's who my family is. It's who I am."

The Academic Senate chair knocked lightly on the door and entered the office. They announced that it was time to begin the processional and start the ceremony.

"I'm nervous," Taylor said. He looked at himself one final time in the floor-length mirror near his office door. He asked for help putting on his doctoral tam. "Thanks for being here. I love you."

"I love you, too, and I have no choice but to be here as the presidential partner and First Gentleman," Dustin said and laughed. "Think of this little investiture event as a dress rehearsal for our wedding at the end of the academic year."

They both grabbed flutes of champagne sitting on a table near the door and clinked glasses. They took one sip and gave each other a quick peck on the lips.

Taylor and Dustin held hands, exited the presidential suite, and eventually made their way down the aisle as the university's orchestra played grand, ceremonial music, and hundreds from the campus community, friends, and family members looked on underneath the sunshine.

Taylor looked forward to shaking up what campus expected of him with the post-investiture campus party. He was, after all, their first Black and Queer campus president. It was going to be an inclusive affair of all groups who'd been made to feel like outsiders in college campus life—D.J. Kidd centering house and R&B music, Manessa, Coco, and their club kid friends doing drag performances and vogueing, the campus and neighborhood high school folklorico groups dancing, some Black and Latinx country music artists, and a Black women's a cappella choir singing old-school music. If campus could have afforded her, they'd have had a show by Beyoncé to cap off the day's festivities—but such was not the case that day.

Indeed, Taylor thought as he and Dustin floated down the main aisle with their friends and admirers looking on, this Presidential Investiture was just a dress rehearsal for what would be happening for them in less than a year at their first, last, and only wedding.

About the Author

Originally from Detroit, Frederick Smith is a graduate of the Missouri School of Journalism, Loyola University Chicago, and Loyola Marymount University. He is the author of *Busy Ain't The Half Of It* (co-authored with Chaz Lamar Cruz), *In Case You Forgot* (co-authored with Chaz Lamar Cruz), *Play It Forward*, *Right Side of the Wrong Bed*, and *Down For Whatever*. He lives in San Francisco.

Books Available From Bold Strokes Books

One and Done by Fredrick Smith. One day can lead to a night of passion…and possibly a chance at love. (978-1-63679-564-5)

Puzzles Can Be Deadly by David S. Pederson. Skip loves a good puzzle. Little does he know that a simple phone call will lead him and his boyfriend Henry to the deadliest puzzle he's ever encountered. (978-1-63679-615-4)

Triad Magic by 'Nathan Burgoine. Face-to-face against forces set in motion hundreds of years ago, Luc, Anders, and Curtis—vampire, demon, and wizard—must draw on the power of blood, soul, and magic to stop a killer. (978-1-63679-505-8)

Head Over Heelflip by Sander Santiago. To secure the biggest prizes at the Colorado Amateur Street Sports Tour, Thomas Jefferson will do almost anything, even marrying his best friend and crush—Arturo "Uno" Ortiz. (978-1-63679-489-1)

Mississippi River Mischief by Greg Herren. When a politician turns up dead and Scotty's client is the most obvious suspect, Scotty and his friends set out to prove his client's innocence. (978-1-63679-353-5)

Murder at the Oasis by David S. Pederson. Palm trees, sunshine, and murder await Mason Adler and his friend Walter as they travel from Phoenix to Palm Springs for what was supposed to be a relaxing vacation but ends up being a trip of mystery and intrigue. (978-1-63679-416-7)

The Speed of Slow Changes by Sander Santiago. As Al and Lucas navigate the ups and downs of their polyamorous relationship, only one thing is certain: romance has never been so crowded. (978-1-63679-329-0)

Manny Porter and The Yuletide Murder by D.C. Robeline. Manny only has the holiday season to discover who killed prominent research scientist Phillip Nikolaidis before the judicial system condemns an innocent man to lethal injection. (978-1-63679-313-9)

Murder at Union Station by David S. Pederson. Private Detective Mason Adler struggles to determine who killed a woman found in a trunk without getting himself killed in the process. (978-1-63679-269-9)

Corpus Calvin by David Swatling. Cloverkist Inn may be haunted, but a ghost materializes from Jason Dekker's past and Calvin's canine instinct kicks in to protect a young boy from mortal danger. (978-1-62639-428-5)

A Champion for Tinker Creek by D.C. Robeline. Lyle James has rescued his dad's auto repair business, but when city hall condemns his neighborhood, Lyle learns only trusting will save his life and help him find love. (978-1-63679-213-2)

Heckin' Lewd: Trans and Nonbinary Erotica, edited by Mx. Nillin Lore. If you want smutty, fearless, gender diverse erotica written by affirming own-voices folks who get it, then this is the book you've been looking for! (978-1-63679-240-8)

Inherit the Lightning by Bud Gundy. Darcy O'Brien and his sisters learn they are about to inherit an immense fortune, but a family mystery about to unravel after seventy years threatens to destroy everything. (978-1-63679-199-9)

Pursued: Lillian's Story by Felice Picano. Fleeing a disastrous marriage to the Lord Exchequer of England, Lillian of Ravenglass reveals an incident-filled, often bizarre, tale of great wealth and power, perfidy, and betrayal. (978-1-63679-197-5)

Murder on Monte Vista by David S. Pederson. Private Detective Mason Adler's angst at turning fifty is forgotten when his "birthday present," the handsome, young Henry Bowtrickle, turns up dead, and it's up to Mason to figure out who did it, and why. (978-1-63679-124-1)

Three Left Turns to Nowhere by Jeffrey Ricker, J. Marshall Freeman & 'Nathan Burgoine. Three strangers heading to a convention in Toronto are stranded in rural Ontario, where a small town with a subtle kind of magic leads each to discover what he's been searching for. (978-1-63679-050-3)

One Verse Multi by Sander Santiago. Life was good: promotion, friends, falling in love, discovering that the multi-verse is on a fast track to collision—wait, what? Good thing Martin King works for a company that can fix the problem, right…um…right? (978-1-63679-069-5)